THE YIN SHEE DRAGON
THE COMPLETE CASES OF MIKE
& TRIXIE, VOLUME 2

THE YIN SHEE
DRAGON
THE COMPLETE CASES OF MIKE
& TRIXIE, VOLUME 2

T.T. FLYNN

ILLUSTRATRATIONS BY
JOSEPH A. FARREN

POPULAR PUBLICATIONS · 2023

TABLE OF CONTENTS

THE YIN SHEE DRAGON

How Could Mike Harris Guess That Killers from East and West Had Joined Forces in the Sleepy Ohio Town Where Yin Shee Offered $300,000 for a Robbery and a Murder?

1

THE BIG BUBBLE

I WAS LUNCHING in the diner an hour and a half east of Toledo when the train secretary rolled along between the tables.

"Mr. Michael Harris!" he pages. "Mr. Michael Harris!"

I stopped him with a toothpick.

"You win the glass cigar-band," I said through some chicken salad. "What wouldst thou with Michael Harris?"

He was slender, dapper; with a coltish face which was shaved and powdered to perfection. The look he handed me was fishy and barbed.

"Are you Mr. Harris?" he questioned acidly.

Dignity, I gathered, he had nothing else but; and I had fractured it. I buttered him with a smile.

"Young man," says I, "I *am* Michael Harris. Let that waiter pass with his tray and tell me your story. What do you want with Michael Harris?"

Not until then did he flourish a telegram at me.

"This was picked up at the last stop," he said coldly. "I've been through eight cars already trying to find you. Almost the whole train."

"Don't tell me you've got a bunion," I cracked as I signed for the wire. "Ever try cutting a piece out of your shoe?"

That finished him. He retired with acid in his soul, and I opened the wire with a prayer in mine.

Broadway was only half a day away—and I feared the worst. I had a vacation coming and Thompson, the big eastern boss of the Blaine Agency, had my vacation on the end of a string which he kept jerking. I couldn't catch up with the big rest. It was beginning to be a headache.

The wire was short and rated an aspirin. It said:

SEE JONATHAN JONES AT INDEPENDENCE
OHIO   THOMPSON

I said, "Damn!" so viciously that two elderly females across the aisle stopped eating and glared at me. I glared back, crammed the wire in my pocket, shoved back the rest of the chicken salad and went back three cars to my seat.

No use wiring Thompson and asking if it were a gag. Thompson didn't gag that way. When he laid business on

I could see the blue circle around his neck where the death-cord had bitten deep.

the line it was business, and the devil take you if you didn't produce without asking fool questions.

The conductor came by. I asked him how to get to Independence, Ohio.

"Change at Cleveland, and take the B. & O. south," he told me.

So I changed at Cleveland and took the B. & O. south.

It was ten minutes after eight that evening when I landed at Independence. I threw my bags in a taxi and told the driver to take me to the best hotel. No vacation in New York rated me the best here in Independence.

I shot out the light overhead, and sprinted toward the bottom of the stairs.

I registered, drew a room on the fourth floor. When I was alone I reached for the telephone directory.

Fourteen Joneses were listed—but only one Jonathan Jones. His address was 2133 Beech Tree Drive. That meant nothing to me. Independence was only a jail so far as I was concerned. The Metropole, where I was staying, was nine stories high, and the cover of the telephone directory gave the population as 43,500.

I called Jonathan Jones. A woman answered, asking my name.

"Harris," I gave her.

It didn't mean anything. "What is it you wish?" she demanded in a suspicious tone. She sounded frightened.

"I wish to talk to Jonathan Jones on an important matter of business," I told her.

"What business?" she came back.

"Madam," I said, "if Jonathan Jones is there, will you call him to the telephone? This isn't a gag."

She hung up on me.

I HUNG UP myself and swore at Thompson, at Independence, Ohio, and at the tribe of Jonathan Jones. With all that off my chest I called the residence again. The same woman answered.

"This is Mr. Harris, calling for Jonathan Jones," I sighed. She said tartly:

"If you won't tell me your business with Mr. Jones, I—"

Her voice shut off. An indistinct murmur came over the wire. Then a deep masculine voice said:

"This is Jonathan Jones speaking."

"I'm Michael Harris from the Blaine Agency."

"Yes, Mr. Harris!" he said quickly. "I've been expecting

you. There was a misunderstanding when you called a few minutes ago. My sister—er—thought you were some one else I'll explain later. I want to see you at once."

"I'll taxi over."

"No!" Jonathan Jones refused curtly. His deep voice carried a ring of command; underlaid, I'd have sworn, with apprehension. "Where are you now?"

"At the Metropole, Room 417."

"I'll be there within thirty minutes. You're registered under your own name, I suppose?"

"Why shouldn't I be?" I countered. No one told me any different."

"I suppose it's all right," he assented dubiously. "Too late to change now; in that hotel anyway. I'll see you in your room."

He hung up and I hung up.

While I opened my bag, washed my face and changed my shirt, I did a lot of thinking. I couldn't figure why Thompson had sidetracked me to this burg so suddenly.

In case we haven't met before, I'm Mike Harris, of the Blaine Agency. We're international, handling all angles of the detective, investigating and protective business. I was on my way back from Chicago, where I'd almost got my liver and lights shot out in a gangster play for society jewels. And now here in Independence, Ohio, I had butted smack into a sweet little mystery. And my vacation was flapping away into the dim distance. So I forgot it and pondered.

Something was behind all that coyness at the other end of the telephone. Jonathan Jones himself had sounded queer. Uneasy, too, because I had registered under my own name. It was plenty mysterious. I wanted to know more about Jonathan Jones. So with a clean bib and tucker under my coat I dropped down into the lobby and bought a cigar.

The smooth brunette at the cigar counter looked intelligent.

"Nice town you have here," I observed.

"It'll do for a dump," she sniffed.

"What's the matter with it?"

"What's the matter with any dump?"

"Soured on life, huh?" I said, biting off the end of the cigar and striking a match. "It must be your feet. Try a pair of Little Wonder shoes."

"You a shoe salesman?" she yawned.

That got her a traveling man's smile.

"I travel, sister. But don't get nervous. I'm not trying to make you. Is there a Jonathan Jones in town?"

Her hand knocked over a pocket tin of tobacco standing on the case. I had all her attention for an instant. Eyes, ears—and a tenseness she could not hide.

"Jonathan Jones?" she repeated sharply. And she seemed to be stalling, saying anything to fill in while her mind wrestled with something else.

"Jonathan Jones," I repeated, nodding. And I grinned at her. "You act like you know somebody by that name, lady," I said.

She set the green tobacco tin upright. Her nails were bright red, long, sharply pointed. I wondered how deep they could furrow a man's face. Her look had been like that. Then it left her as quickly as it had come. She was sleepy, yawning, disinterested again; all but her eyes. From under half-closed lids, she was watching me.

Why should a simple little question like that jar her so?

Don't ask me. I couldn't figure it. And her reply jarred me almost as bad.

"Jonathan Jones?" says she vaguely. "You mean the rich guy who owns the Jones Soap Company? That Jonathan Jones?"

There was only one Jonathan Jones in the telephone directory, so I nodded.

"The same, sister. Know him?"

She sniffed.

"How would I be knowing him? He's worth a couple of million. I ain't in his class. What's the gag? Does he wear Little Wonder shoes?"

"If he doesn't, he should," I chuckled. "How about some poker dice for a fistful of cigars?"

She shrugged; reached for the leather cup. And while we shook I tried to get her going again. But no talkee. That brunette clammed up like nobody's business. She wasn't mad, but she wasn't interested and let me see it.

The dice rolled for her. I paid and wandered back to my room. I had plenty more to think about now. So Jonathan Jones owned the Jones Soap Company? I'd never heard of it, but that meant nothing. Soap and suds had evidently done well by Jonathan. Worth a couple of millions. He was a big bubble. And over the telephone he had sounded as if something had jarred him plenty. It began to look as if there might be something to this after all.

Jonathan Jones was late. I waited until he was an hour overdue and then telephoned his house again. A Swedish accent answered this time.

"Is Jonathan Jones there?" I asked wearily.

"He bane gone."

"Where bane he gone to?"

"Mr. Jones bane Mercy Hospital," she told me, and hung up.

2

MUMBLED WARNINGS

FIVE MINUTES LATER I was in a taxi rolling toward Jonathan Jones. I had telephoned to the Mercy Hospital. Reluctant to talk, they finally had admitted that Jonathan Jones had been injured in an automobile accident and was there, conscious.

In the hushed lobby of the hospital a nurse, starched but septic, demanded my business with Mr. Jones. She eyed me with suspicion, but when I insisted she finally sent a nurse to Jones's room with my name. Her manner indicated that it wouldn't do any good, but I might as well be humored. I gathered that Jonathan Jones was majesty himself around the hospital.

A moment later I had the reason. A brass plate set in the wall read:

THE ALICIA JONES MEMORIAL WING

Jones must have had second sight when he donated the wing.

My welcome warmed up when the nurse returned with instructions for me to go up at once. She guided me to the second floor. Just before we reached Jones's room two women came out and passed us in the hall. The older one looked at me sharply. She had a solid, substantial face and a tight, severe mouth. Later I found out she was the sharp-tongued female who had first talked to me over the tele-phone.

But the other! Sweet, sweet peas!

She was about eighteen, and rated at least the front row in the "Vanities." I'm red-headed and not too large. She just matched me in height, and was slender and cuddly. The little brown suit she wore never came from Independence, Ohio. Paris labels were sewn in it if I could judge style. Her hat was the same; simple, expensive, chic in every line.

Sun tan was soft on her small, oval face as she barely glanced at me from big, wide eyes. Any other time they would have begged for attention. But now they were red from weeping and weren't interested.

The two women went out. The nurse ushered me into Jonathan Jones's room, closed the door behind me, and went her way. And I stood there in the quiet, dimly-lighted room with the smell of antiseptics strong and heavy about me.

In the white, enameled bed across the room Jonathan Jones lay. A nurse turned from the bed and came noiselessly to me on rubber heels.

Cute, too; but she was serious. Her low voice was disap-proving.

"Mr. Jones insisted on seeing you," she said under her breath, "but will you make it as brief as possible? He is in no condition to see anyone for a day or so. He is suffering greatly from the shock and—er—delusions."

The last she slipped me in a furtive whisper, with a half-glance over her shoulder, as if afraid she might be over-heard.

"Doctor Schmidt," she said, louder, "this is the gentle-man."

The M.D. turned, grunting something and scowling at me.

Beyond him I saw the slender figure of a man under the white bed sheet. At least I guessed it was a man. All I could see above the sheet were white strips of bandage. Arms, neck, face, and the top of his head were swathed. Mouth, nose, eyes, and a little of his hair were all that were visible.

But he heard us.

With a groan, an abrupt summoning of effort he came up on an elbow. Through the holes in the bandage two burning eyes peered at me. They were clouded. They seemed to grope through a mental fog, trying to find me and focus.

"Harris?" Jonathan Jones whispered. His voice was harsh, but weak, pitifully weak for all the effort it cost him. I stepped over to the bed.

"I'm Harris," I said. "I got here as soon as I heard about it. Anything I can do?"

He was panting from the effort. His groping eyes shifted to the doctor.

"Get out!" he whispered.

"Please, Mr. Jones!" the M.D. begged hastily. "This won't do at all. Lie down."

"Get out, damn you! Both of you!"

All man, this slender, wiry Jonathan Jones; half dead, hanging to consciousness with an effort, he smashed an iron will against the quiet of the room with only a whis-per—and got his way.

The doctor gave me a final frown, turned, nodded curtly to the nurse, and stepped out into the hall with her.

Jonathan Jones held himself there on his elbow for a moment while his eyes groped for me. A visible breath of relief, and he sank on the pillow, muttering in a low mono-tone. I had to lean close to get it.

"Glad… see you," he muttered. "Hope… they sent… good man. Need one. Truck smashed car. Wasn't—acci-dent. Deliberate."

Jonathan Jones paused, breathing stertorously through the bandages.

I leaned closer. "A truck cracked you deliberately?" I said.

"Yes." It was only a breath.

"Why?" I asked him quickly.

"Knew… where I was going… I think," Jones said pain-fully. "Tried… stop…" His voice trailed away. Eyes closed, he lay still and seemed to have forgotten me.

Jonathan Jones was a sick man; but I had to know more. I bent over him.

"Who did it? Why'd they want to stop you? What did you want me for?" I asked carefully.

MAYBE HE HEARD me. Maybe he knew he would not have time to answer. He didn't anyway. He tried to lift his head and couldn't make it. Under the sheet I could see his hands lifting slightly, clenching with effort.

His head rolled on the pillow toward me. Through the white layer of bandages his trembling whisper reached out to me.

"Tonight… Golden Dragon… both of them… suspect.…"

I leaned closer, trying to pick those illusive mutterings out of the air. But his voice trailed away, was lost in the bandages. He lay still and seemed to have stopped breathing.

"Mr. Jones!" I said sharply.

He lay there like one dead.

I made for the door. The doctor and nurse were in the hall.

"You'd better look at him," I told them.

The M.D. brushed by me, caught Jones's wrist and felt with practiced fingers for the pulse.

"Miss Carson, the hypodermic!" he snapped. And, as she flitted to a table against the wall, he threw to me:

"I knew he should not have seen anyone else! Good night!"

I left, puzzled, disturbed, mystified. I was getting nowhere rapidly. Jones only had made it worse.

On his way out to see me, his automobile had been struck by a truck. Deliberately. He seemed certain of that. Some one had tried to keep him from seeing me.

A thing like that had to be planned. You couldn't plant a trick where a man would pass, without knowing a lot. No one knew I was in town. No one knew Jones was coming to see me, unless it was that severe, tight-mouthed woman who had answered the telephone. Jones's sister. She couldn't have sold him out.

And then Jones's last words!

It wasn't reasonable. It wasn't sensible. Jones—a hard-headed soap manufacturer—had mumbled of a Golden Dragon. Chewing it over I made the hospital lobby just in time to hear a stocky, thick-shouldered young man speaking to the brisk nurse behind the desk.

"But I'm Adrian Jones, his nephew. I have a right to see him. My aunt and my cousin were just up there."

"I'm sorry, Mr. Jones, you can't," the nurse said. "The doctor just telephoned orders that no one else be allowed in his room tonight. His condition is serious."

"How serious? Will—will he live?" the young man demanded.

Cupping a lighter to my cigarette, I took it all in, and Adrian Jones too—from black, curly hair; tenderly arranged above a broad forehead, down to a straight nose, a wide, sulky mouth, to a chin that was weak as the hair.

The nurse answered without emotion.

"We can't tell, Mr. Jones. Everything possible is being done for your uncle. We will be glad to answer telephone inquiries about his condition. Perhaps this gentleman can tell you something. He has just come down from the room."

Adrian Jones swung toward me, frowning slightly.

"I don't think I know you," he said to me. "I'm Adrian Jones. I'm trying to find out how my uncle is."

"The name," I said, "is Harris. Your uncle's in a bad way. He was unconscious when I left."

"D'you think he'll die?" he asked—and stood there biting his lower lip while he waited for my reply.

I shrugged and thought I'd hate to have anyone so interested in my death. If he'd asked if Jones would live, it would have been different.

"I can't tell you a thing about him," I said. "I'm no doctor. He seems to be hurt pretty bad."

Behind his frown, young Adrian Jones was studying me.

A peculiar expression was in his eyes. His back was in the light. I couldn't make him out.

"You're a stranger in town, aren't you, Mr. Harris? I don't recall seeing you before, or hearing my uncle speak of you."

It was more than curiosity. Strained eagerness was behind that question. I looked at him blandly, answered blandly:

"Your uncle probably knows a lot of people you don't."

"It's queer you knew he was here so soon after the accident," he persisted.

"Isn't it?" I agreed.

We had walked to the front door by then. I opened it, walked outside with him and asked a question of my own.

"Do you live with Mr. Jones, young man?"

He was about twenty-three. I was only six years older, but I'd been through the mill. He was soft; soft as those black curls over which he now clapped an expensive hat.

"I live at the house part of the time," he answered readily enough. "Glad to have met you, Mr. Harris."

Without offering to shake hands he ran down the steps and jumped into a long, racy roadster with the top laid down. A girl was waiting for him. I heard her voice raised in querulous disapproval as he sent the car racing down the street. She wasn't the same type as the little beauty who had emerged from Jonathan Jones's room.

My taxi was waiting where I had left it. The driver reached back, opened the door and I got in.

"Back to the hotel," I said.

I tripped over a pair of feet. Some one shoved a gun in my ribs. Hands caught me, pulled me down on the seat. The taxi started with a jerk.

3

THUGS ON THE ROAD

WHEN A GUN hits your ribs, when you're manhandled, kidnaped, there's only one answer. Trouble. I didn't fight. It wouldn't have done any good.

"I'll bite," I said, scrouging into a more comfortable position. "What's the answer?"

A man sat on each side of me. I couldn't make out their faces in the black shadows. Each of them had a hand on one of my arms, and the gun was still there, boring into my ribs, ready for action.

"Shut up!" a gruff voice ordered at my right.

"Never mind stabbing me with that rod," I said. "I can take a hint."

The man on my left had the gun. He screwed it in deeper. It hurt. I drew a deep breath. Guns weren't new. I'd been in tight spots before and gotten out of them. I wasn't yellow. I was willing to take the cards as they fell.

But this was different.

It wasn't on the cards. I didn't know what it was all about. By rights no one should have known I was coming to the hospital. No one had known I had gone there. It was all as mysterious as Jonathan Jones's accident. And it looked fully as dangerous.

I tried again, mildly. "How about you two giving me an idea about all this? You've got the wrong man, haven't you?"

"Your name's Harris, ain't it?" the gruff one on my right grunted.

"Guilty."

"We got the right guy, then."

"What have you got him for?"

"Shut up!"

And there I was—and there they were. I felt like a kid being whipped for the candy some one else had stolen.

The taxi was rolling fast, turning a corner now and then, but heading in one general direction. We reached the edge of town and kept on out into the country. As the last street light fell behind and the black, lonely countryside opened up about us I began to feel queer.

"What are you guys doing, taking me for a ride?" I burst out finally.

That drew me a cuff on the side of the jaw.

From then on I saw red, but there was nothing I could do about it. The taxi turned suddenly off into a dirt road, and stopped out of sight of the highway. Every move must have been prearranged.

"Get out!" the gruff voice at my right said.

He opened the door, climbed out ahead of me, and waited.

Without seeing it, I knew he had a gun in his hand as he waited there. He grabbed my arm as I came out, and the gun gouged my side while the driver and the other man got out, too.

The night lay black, heavy about us. Somewhere nearby frogs were booming. The dim car lights showed red clay ruts ahead of the car. They were the only lights in any direction.

The three men gathered about me. They were all taller, heavier than I was. I found myself wondering who would shoot first. Heavenly halls looked mighty near at that moment.

But it wasn't heavenly halls I drew. A fist smashed into my face. I reeled and ran smack into another punch that knocked me dizzy. Before I could get my hands up the three of them were beating me.

It was terrible. I'd never been mobbed like that. I was dizzy, groggy, half out, helpless, before I realized what was happening. I didn't have sense enough to fall down until I collapsed, half unconscious. And, as I lay on the ground, they kicked me.

Far, far off the gruff voice snarled:

"That's what we do to nosy dicks who come sneaking in where they ain't wanted! How d'you like it?"

I groaned. It was all I could do.

And they kicked me some more. The gruff voice came floating out of the distance again:

"This is only a sample of what you get if you don't take the next train out of town. You ain't wanted here."

They kicked me a few more times for luck and jumped back into the taxi. It turned there in the road, raced back past me toward the highway.

By the time I was able to raise myself to my hands the tail-lights were vanishing around a turn.

The warm, salty taste of blood was in my mouth. The inside of my lip had been cut badly against a tooth. My face felt as if it had been run through a meat grinder. I

ached all over. When I tried to get up I staggered and fell down again.

It was some minutes before I could start walking, still staggering dizzily. And, as I walked, I began to swear, getting madder each step.

I was used to rough stuff. I'd stuck a gun in a man's ribs and threatened to kill him—and meant it. But this was too raw; this was cowardly, yellow. I hadn't had a chance from the first. Three of them!

Before I reached the highway I made a bitter vow that a gun would go under my arm the minute I got back to the hotel and stay there until I'd torn this mystery apart and settled with those three who had beaten me up. They'd have to kill me to stop me—and I'd kill them first if I could.

I HAD TO walk almost to the city limits before I got a ride. A milkwagon driver picked me up and dropped me a block from the hotel. A look in the little mirror of a slot machine made me wilder than ever. I had a beautiful black eye. Blood was smeared at the corner of my mouth. My cheek was cut, my face was bruised, my clothes looked as if I'd been wallowing all over the road.

I tidied myself a little and walked into the hotel, cold mad.

The smooth brunette was still behind the cigar counter. She looked at me and smiled as if she got a kick out of it.

"It must have been some party, mister," she gave me across the counter. "I'll bet you weren't demonstrating Little Wonder shoes."

I forced a grin as I stopped and lighted a cigarette.

"Would you believe I ran into a door?" I said.

"If you did, it was a revolving door," she came back,

eyeing me with cool amusement. She yawned at me from behind the long, sharp, red finger nails. "That's what you smart birds get for running wild in a small town."

I inhaled my cigarette and looked her over with interest. And right there I decided I didn't like her. She wouldn't have been so calm if she'd known what was going on in my mind. She was the only person in town who had known I was interested in Jonathan Jones. Standing there, I wondered if she had anything to do with what had happened. I was still wondering when I turned toward the elevator without replying to her last crack. She couldn't have known about the telephone call to the hospital.

In my bedroom I surveyed the damage more carefully. The cut on my lip had stopped bleeding. My eye was a beauty. Many bruises that I could feel were not visible. But one thing was visible—a peculiar triangle-shaped mark on my right cheek. Something had struck there heavily. A ring, I suspected, with a triangle-shaped setting.

I washed and went down to the nearest drug store, bought a black patch for my eye, and, with a handful of quarters, entered a telephone booth and called New York. I called Thompson's house, where he was most apt to be this time of the evening. Thompson answered.

"This is Mike Harris," I said. "I'm in Independence, Ohio."

"Fine!" Thompson came back heartily. "Got the situation well in hand, I suppose?"

"What situation?" I yelped. "What's this all about, anyway? The man you sent me to is in the hospital unconscious. Somebody tried to kill him with a truck. And I've just been snatched out into the country and got the hell beaten out of me and warned to get out of town!"

Thompson's whistle of amazement was plain over the wire.

"Strange," Thompson said.

"Strange!" I choked. "Is that all you've got to say about it? What am I doing here? I don't know any more now than when I got your wire on the Chicago train."

"You do," Thompson came back. "You know there's danger there. Watch your step, Mike."

"I've already fallen on my face!" I told him bitterly. "I called you up to find out what I'm up against. With Jones unconscious, I'm in the dark."

"I can't tell you a thing, Mike," Thompson said. "This Jones telephoned me a few minutes before I wired you. He seemed greatly disturbed. He said he knew one of our men in the Singapore office, and he had a job for us. He asked for one of our best operators to come at once. The expense account is wide open. You can have as many men as you need. That's all I know."

"A fat lot of help you are," I grumbled.

"It's up to you, Mike," Thompson spoke cheerfully from the safety of his home. "Handle it any way you see fit. But be careful. Don't let anything happen to you."

I cursed him and hung up.

Over the telephone I ordered a taxi to meet me in front of the drug store. When it came I had myself driven to the house of Jonathan Jones. Some one there, I reasoned, should be able to give me a little more information.

Jonathan Jones lived in the northwest section, on a hill. The driveway wound up to the house between big trees. The house itself was brick; severe, substantial. One could visualize generations of Joneses living and dying here while the factory turned out a never-ending stream of soap. Wealthy, dull; this Jones family.

And that only shrouded the events of the evening in more mystery.

Curtained windows glowed with light. Two automobiles were standing in front of the house. One, a taxi, had arrived first. It stood in front of a black Chevrolet sedan—the same kind of a taxi that had carried me out into the country.

"Wait for me," I said to my driver, and walked forward to the other hack, sliding a hand under my arm where a hard automatic snuggled comfortingly. Plenty of cabs in town looked like this one—but I wasn't taking chances. I was taxi-conscious since being trapped in one of the same brand.

The driver was lounging behind the wheel, half asleep, I judged by the limp way his arm hung out the window and the relaxed angle of his head. He did not look up as I came to the door.

"Hello," I said.

Still he did not look up. His eyes were closed; I'd not have been surprised to hear him snoring—except that about him there was no indication of breathing.

I bent closer to speak again—and didn't. In the glare of my own cab's headlights I saw a little trickle of fresh red blood seeping down from under his cap. Spreading red fingers to front and back of his ear, it had dripped down to form a small damp spot on the shoulders of his coat. His cap had been bashed in by the impact of some heavy object.

4

THE RUSTLING OF DEATH

INSTINCT WHIPPED THE automatic out into my hand, sent me back a step while I looked around quickly, and then into the back of the cab. The rear seat was empty. I had made sure the Chevrolet sedan was empty when I passed it.

Peacefully those two cars stood there. Quietly the house loomed behind them. The spot was so still I could hear the breeze rustling through the upper branches of the trees; rustling like some alien thing passing through the black night overhead. Like death, perhaps, passing from the spot where it had been disturbed.

A silly idea? I've heard of sillier. There was the driver slumped in an attitude of death. Jonathan Jones lay on his hospital bed very close to death. I hadn't been far from it myself this evening.

No, not so silly.

The wrist hanging from the window of the car was limp when I lifted it. Seconds passed before I located the faintest, weakest of pulses and drew a breath of relief.

My driver was coming cautiously toward me. Young, stocky, open faced, his voice had an edge of excitement.

"Anything wrong? I seen you draw that gun," he called as he came.

"This man has been slugged."

He came to my side, looked, whistled softly, glanced quickly around as I had.

"Somethin' wrong here!" he exclaimed under his breath. "We better beat it an' get a cop!"

"I'll call up from inside the house. They'll have a telephone."

He gave me a sharp look. "Hell, don't you know?" he asked. "Ain't you been in the house before?"

"No. But I'm going in now."

"Listen, mister, pay me the six-bits meter charge! I'm leaving!" he said hurriedly. "I don't know what this is all about—but I don't want none of it! I got a family to support and I can't get tied up in any trouble!"

I gave him a dollar, told him to keep the change. He ran back to his cab, started the motor, and slowed his rush of departure as he came abreast of me.

"Sure you don't want to go?" he urged from behind the wheel.

"No."

"I'll phone headquarters, then."

And he drove furiously away, leaving me standing in the driveway watching the receding red tail lights. For an instant I felt mighty alone. The grounds, the lighted house, were so quiet. The noise of our arrival hadn't drawn anyone out. The house seemed to brood there, all lighted and alive, waiting for me to do something.

The palm of my hand was moist about the automatic as I walked on the front porch in the grip of that feeling. My nerves were crawling. Not exactly fear. More tension and the certainty that there was going to be more of this—and uncertainty as to what it would be.

THE FRONT DOOR was standing open perhaps six inches. I listened for some sound inside. There wasn't any. I put a hand against the door to push—and froze there. Just inside the door, against the wall, a man was sitting in a chair looking out at me.

Without movement he sat there in that tense, electric quiet—and his eyeballs were bulging out, his tongue was protruding from between his lips, and his face was twisted, set in a ghastly purplish mask of fear and horror. He was sitting stiffly upright against the back of the chair, arms rigid on the chair arms.

Scalp crawling, I stood rooted to the spot. I knew death. *This* was death, with horror and violence thrown in for good measure. And the silence, that damnable silence, bore down like a shroud of threat.

I had to go in. I couldn't have done anything else. But it was hard. Me, Mike Harris, finding it hard, when I was credited with steel nerves and an utter lack of fear! Maybe the beating I had gotten had given me the jitters. Anyway, I went in watchfully, warily.

That saved my life.

He had been waiting just inside the door—that slender, crouching man who, as I stepped in, bounced at me with the savage quickness of an uncoiling steel spring. I only glimpsed the vague blur of movement, the upraised arm with the leather-covered sap, the thin, dark face showing white teeth in a snarl—and I surprised him.

Instead of dodging, ducking, retreating, I was on him instantly.

We met with a shock which stopped us both; but I was under the downswing of that leather-covered black-jack. It shaved my head, smashed into the back of my left shoulder—and I struck up with the automatic at the same instant.

I could have shot him—but it would have made noise. I didn't want noise. Square on the side of the face, on his cheekbone and temple, I slammed the automatic with all the weight of my body behind it. He went down without a sound.

My shoulder was half numb from his blow. My nerves were suddenly all right, though. This was action, this was something to work on. I didn't have to wait for phantoms to flit and strike out of the threatening, brooding silence. Breathing hard, I stood there for long seconds; watchful, listening.

The dead man in the chair faced me not an arm's length away, as ghastly as ever. But he didn't matter now. He was only a man, dead, harmless, even though he had died as I never want to die. He had been garroted. I could see the blue-black circle around his neck where the death-cord had bitten deep. Life and speech must have been choked off instantly with one savage twist.

He was over forty, and looked like a man servant. Had enough size and brawn for him to have given a better account of himself. I wondered if the man who lay at my feet had done it. Slender, dark-skinned, with a prominent, high-bridged nose, a thin, cruel mouth and sleek black hair, hardly mussed even now, he was a foreigner. The Orient was the first thing I thought of—and then almost instantly

Jonathan Jones's mention of our Singapore office came to mind.

From inside his coat I took several papers; and was straightening up with them when I was almost deafened by the sudden crash of a shot. Behind me door glass shattered as the bullet smashed through.

5

THE BATTLE ON THE STAIRS

I WAS CLEAR across the hall before I stopped moving. A second shot followed me, raking the side of my coat, thudding into the floor. They were coming from the top of the wide, curving stairs. I glimpsed the snout of a gun resting on the stair railing where it met the ceiling line, and behind the muzzle a set, peering face sighting at me for the third time.

In that lighted hall I was a perfect target. I didn't have a chance to get out before he put a bullet in me. I shot out the light overhead, and sprinted through the shower of glass toward the bottom of the stairs as he fired again and again.

His gun was almost empty and mine was full. That thought was some comfort as I threw myself up the stairs, dodging from side to side, praying that in the dark he'd miss again. And doubting it. Luck couldn't hold forever.

The stench of burnt powder was strong. The shot had deafened me. I couldn't hear my own steps. But I charged up the curved stairs pumping two shots at the spot where the man had been crouching.

No shots came back. He wasn't there. I plunged into the dark upper hall, certain a gun was waiting just ahead.

Silence pressed at my ringing ears. I slapped a hand at the wall, found a light switch, pressed it.

The hall was empty.

Its spacious, peaceful length gave me the feeling that I might have dreamed everything. Here was only peace, comfort, security. Starting at the front, I worked back, opening each door—expecting a shot each time.

And when I opened the fourth door and clicked the light switch, I jumped, swearing under my breath. Two women were on the bed inside. One was sitting up, the other lying down. Both were tied, gagged. The one sitting, with her legs over the edge of the bed, shrank back as the light went on. Her eyes were wide, dark with fright for a moment as she stared. Then relief showed on her sun-tanned cheeks.

She tried to say something behind the gag and couldn't. I had it off a moment later. Huskily she said, "Thank you."

"Yeah," I gave her gruffly, working at the light, strong cord about her wrists. "What happened?"

I had spotted her for a thoroughbred in the hospital corridor, this slender, cuddly girl of about eighteen, with her big, wide eyes. She came through now, steadily, calmly as I freed her.

"I don't know how they got in," she said. "They were up here before I knew it. They tied Aunt Emma and myself and threatened to kill us if we made any sound. And then they went back to Uncle John's study, I think. They—they didn't seem to be in any hurry."

"Who were they?"

"I never saw them before. What is the matter with your

eye and your face?" she asked me calmly as she lifted her ankles and I tackled the cords there.

"Ran into some trouble," I grunted. "Who are you?"

"Why, I'm Nan Brewster. I thought you knew."

"How should I know?"

"I saw you going into Uncle John's room at the hospital. And—and what are you doing here now? Who was firing those shots? Aunt Emma fainted when they started."

"Best place for her," I cracked. "Here, stand up." I helped her. "How many men were here?" I asked as her hand rested on my arm.

"Two is all I saw or heard," she replied, after hesitating a moment.

"Is there any other way to get downstairs besides the front stairs?"

"No," she said. And added anxiously, with her eyes big and wide, "Did those shots hurt anyone?"

"I'm afraid not," I grunted. I was getting irritated. "We might have been at a pink tea. Stay here and look after the old lady!" I snapped. "I've got business to do."

I headed for the back of the hall, skipping the rest of the rooms. The last room on the right was the one I wanted.

The door opened readily enough, showing a lighted study. And had it been ransacked? It had! A whirlwind had gone through there in a hurry. Shelves of books had been tossed on the floor, pictures yanked down from the walls, the drawers of a desk emptied on the floor. Even the rug had been hauled up at the corners and left that way. A window at the back of the room was up from the bottom.

I looked out, saw the roof of a rear porch outside—and at

the same moment heard an automobile motor racing at the front of the house. A car was moving down the driveway.

Swearing, I went out of that room with a can on my tail, raced along the hall, tumbled down the stairs, and swore harder than ever before I reached the bottom.

The man I had knocked out in the front hall was gone. Only the corpse was there in the chair, stiff and stark, staring at the partly opened door as if horrified at what it had seen go out that way.

And I ran outside with the little hope. Right! The Chevrolet sedan was gone. While I had been untying that big-eyed girl with the sun-tanned cheeks, the man I wanted had gone out the back window; out the window over the porch, down to the ground, and around the house to the car. And the man in the front hall had either recovered consciousness and walked out to the car or been carried out.

The taxi was still there with its unconscious driver.

YOU COULD HAVE had me for two nickels or a plugged dime as I ran back upstairs. The old lady was sitting up on the bed fanning herself with a limp hand when I burst into the bedroom. She squawked and almost went down again.

"It's all right, Aunty," Nan Brewster said soothing, waving a bottle of smelling-salts under aunty's schnozzle. "He's—he's—" She broke off and turned to me. "Just what are you?" she asked, big-eyed.

"Me? I'm the Pasha of Zanzibar!" I snarled. "And like always happens, women have balled up the party! Are you two sure you don't know anything about this? You don't know those fellows or what they were here for?"

Her eyes were wide, wide—two dark pools that could

drown the sense
out of any ordi-
nary man, as they
seemed to be trying
to drown it out of
me at the moment.

"Why no," she
says, all hurry and
vague. "How could
I know anything
about them? Didn't
I tell you I—I never
have seen either of them before?"

Trixie Meehan

And the old lady, filling her face with a whoosh of the
smelling-salts, gave me a glare that would have peeled the
plating off a chromium radiator.

"My good man," she says, "what do you mean by bursting in here this way and speaking so? Of course, we know
nothing about this! Are you a member of the police force?"

"No, but I'm a member in good standing of the Brother-
hood of Man," I yelped at her. "The cops have been notified and I'm trying to find out all I can before they get
here. I'm working for Jonathan Jones. I'm the man who
telephoned here earlier in the evening for him. That's not
to get out—you understand? Both of you!"

The old lady sniffed.

Nan Brewster started. I could feel her freezing up on me.
I'd sensed it before I spoke. She was a swell little actress—
only her eyes didn't register. She had been covering up.
She was now. She knew something I didn't know, and she
wasn't going to tell me.

And I wasn't going to let her get away with it.

"Come on!" I said, roughly. "You know something about this. I've had dames try to back and fill on me before. Let's have it."

Michael Harris

It wasn't the way to handle her, of course. I doubt if ever in her life she had been spoken to that way before. Her eyes filled, as if she was going to weep. But she grew scornful instead.

"I've told you all I have to say."

"Yah? Maybe you'll tell the police more. This is murder, you know. There's a man down in the hall deader than the League of Nations!"

"Smith? Dead?" she gasped. And this time her eyes were really wide. The sun-tan couldn't cover up the pallor that came on her face. Her hand went to her throat. She stared at me with unfeigned horror.

"Smith or Jones or Black or White," I gave her back. "He's there and he's dead!"

"Oh, my God!" squawks the old lady, and keels over limper than an eel on a butcher's counter.

Nan Brewster faced me, fighting for self control. Her little hands were clenched tight at her sides and there were really tears in those big dark eyes now. Her voice quavered, came out with an effort.

"Smith is the b-butler," she gulped. "Are you sure he's dead?"

"Lady," says I, "I'm practically sure. I can spot 'em in the dark by now. He's not only dead but he's going to stay dead. And you know something about it. You'd better come through. I'm here to help you. I'm drawing my money from your uncle. The police aren't, and they won't be in a lather to help anyone."

"I believe you're telling the truth," she whispered.

"Sure I am. And what *is* the truth?"

"Why—why—"

I waited for it. She was going to talk—and suddenly she wasn't. I saw it in her eyes, first, and then in the quick firming of her jaws.

"I don't know anything," she got out with a husky effort that showed her heart was in it. "Have you done anything about the young woman downstairs?"

"What young woman?"

"Why, the one that's down there in the drawing room."

"You don't tell me," I gave her sarcastically. "Why didn't you say so before? Who came in that taxi outside?"

"She did. She wanted to see Uncle John. She's from the advertising agency that handles the factory account. She was very insistent, according to Smith. She said she had just come from out of town on very important business. Smith came up and told us, and then went back to tell her I would be down in a few minutes. And before I could get down those two men came up here—and tied us."

"And that reminds me," I said as I went out to the door. "Where's the Swede maid who answered the telephone this evening?"

"This is Hulda's evening off. She left as soon as we returned from the hospital."

"And probably saved her neck," I left behind as I hit the hall. "Anyone as dumb as she sounded would have gotten in bad tonight."

I went down the stairs with a rush, gun still in my hand, looking for the young woman who had been on the spot when murder had been committed.

The drawing room was dark. I found the light switch inside the door and pressed it. At first glance I was ready to swear she wasn't in the room.

And then I saw her feet on the floor at the end of a big overstuffed couch which must have gotten into this severe, stiff house by mistake. Her feet on the floor! I went forward to inspect the body.

And the body came to life and sat up with an effort when I appeared.

"Trixie!" I yelped.

She gargled something behind a gag. It was Trixie Meehan from the Blaine Agency.

6

MIKE GETS SOME HELP

IN ALL THE wide world there was only one little package of dynamite like Trixie Meehan. She would have rattled around in a thimble, but what there was of her was tough, quick, brainy and brave.

Trixie Meehan would tackle anything and she usually tackled it right. She had a face like a cute little innocent and a tongue dipped in acid. And whenever she got within speaking distance of me she started riding me, which was too often. Somehow or other she was always turning up on cases where I was assigned. We had parted fervently and profanely in Chicago a couple of days before. She should have been in New York by now—and here she was smack in the middle of death and mystery in this little Ohio town.

And she ran true to form.

"You big ape!" Trixie choked as the gag came out of her mouth. "What do you mean by leaving me stretched out all over the floor here while you gallop over the house swearing in your beard?"

"I didn't hear you. What're you doing here?"

"What do you think I'm doing here? Thompson sent me. And while I was sitting here trying to get in touch with Jones, a man walked in and did this to me. And you run around shooting guns and paying no attention to me when I call you through that gag. Mike, are you hurt?"

I was helping her on her feet by then. Trixie's voice had softened with anxiety.

"Nothing wrong with me."

"I was afraid so!" she snapped. She put her little hands on her hips and glared up at me. "I heard you go up those steps, Mike Harris! Just as if there was nothing at the top. Why—why do you take chances like that?"

"I'll bite, now that you ask it. Why?"

"Because you're dumb!" Trixie flared. "What's this all about, anyway? What were those three men doing here?"

"Three men?"

"You heard me."

"There were only two men."

"Three men," said Trixie positively. "I heard three different voices. Two of them went upstairs and the other went out on the front porch. He didn't—"

Trixie stopped speaking. Her left eye drooped in a warning signal.

I turned, and from the doorway Nan Brewster said:

"I see you found her."

There she was, with the dead man behind her, acting as calm and cool as you please while she looked at us and walked slowly into the room.

"I didn't know you two knew each other," she said, looking from Trixie to me.

Trixie looked back at her as only Trixie Meehan can, a bit icy.

"Who said we did?" Trixie asked.

"Why, I don't know. I thought… Nan Brewster bit her

lip. She was young, but oddly mature, too. "You seemed to be talking as if you knew each other," she finished.

"I'd talk to any man who took a gag out of my mouth and untied me," Trixie said. "What has happened here? I was sitting on the couch when two men came in and seized me."

"I don't know," Nan Brewster replied.

"Then you better find out," Trixie informed her tartly. "Where is Mr. Jones?"

"He isn't here. I'm Nan Brewster, his niece. What was it you wanted, please? I was informed you were here from the advertising agency. Isn't this a rather unusual time to be transacting business? Uncle John always keeps his business at the office."

I knew Trixie well enough to spot the slight glow of admiration in her eyes. Nan Brewster was conducting herself with amazing poise.

"I just got into town this evening," Trixie explained more gently. "It was important that I see your uncle at once."

"You can't," said Nan Brewster. "He is in the hospital after a bad automobile accident this evening."

"I'm sorry," Trixie sighed. "I'll have to wait, then."

"I'm sure some one at the plant can see you," Nan Brewster suggested.

"I'm afraid not. I'm here to see Mr. Jones personally."

Nan Brewster regarded her speculatively.

"I thought I heard you say something about three voices—Miss Meehan, isn't it?"

"It is," said Trixie guilessly. "And you did. I was telling this gentleman I thought I heard three men speaking."

"Did you hear what they said?"

"No," Trixie denied without batting an eyelash.

"I'm sure there were only two men. I saw them," Nan Brewster told her sweetly.

"You must be right," says Trixie just as sweetly.

I HAD THE lead I wanted. Little Miss Nan Brewster was covering up for the third man. She knew who he was. She didn't want his identity known. It hit me like a shot—was Nan Brewster the one who had made it possible for the truck to smash into Jonathan Jones? Into her own uncle?

"Were you here in the house when your uncle drove off this evening?" I asked her.

Her answer was guarded. "I was. Why?"

Before I could answer, a police siren wailed up the driveway toward the house. The taxi driver had really notified the cops.

"Last chance," I threw at Nan Brewster. "Anything to say?"

Wide-eyed, innocent as ever, she came back at me. "No. What would I say?"

"Something about the Golden Dragon? I cracked at her—and watched her face closely.

She looked vague.

"I don't understand."

"Never mind. You will."

I went out front as a patrol car pulled to a stop. The two coppers who hopped out were nervous, loaded for danger. They charged at me with drawn revolvers.

"What's the trouble here? That the car with the murdered man?" the first one yelped, throwing an arm at the taxi.

"Inside, boys," I invited. "That hacker will come out of it all right."

They breasted the steps, giving me the eye. The lead one could have made two of me. He had a whisky nose, red and mottled, and his eyebrows were thick, black and scowling.

"You the guy who came here in the taxi?" he snorted, towering over me.

"Check. Come in and see the body. It's worth the trip out here."

They barged into the doorway. Their eyes popped. Fingering their guns they looked at the body, at me, and at Nan Brewster and Trixie Meehan. The second copper, thin, raw-boned, lantern-jawed, tight-mouthed, barked at me:

"Who did this? What's it all about? Who are you?"

"Don't ask," I said. "I just dropped in. Harris is the name. I came to see Jonathan Jones and met an execution squad."

I told them what happened.

"Perhaps Miss Brewster can tell you more," I finished. "She was here. Miss Meehan, the other young lady, walked into trouble just like I did."

Nan Brewster spoke calmly. "I don't know anything about it. The motive seems to have been robbery."

She looked at the body, shuddered slightly. The coppers missed it.

"Better call a doctor for the hacker out there," I said. "I didn't get around to it, what with dodging lead and untying females all over the house."

"An ambulance is coming," the big fellow growled. He peered at the butler with a wise air. "Choked to death," he announced solemnly.

"And the study upstairs was ransacked, the women were

tied up, the hacker slugged, and half a dozen shots fired at me," I finished. "Untangle all that and you'll have the answer."

The big fellow removed his cap and scratched his head.

"Looks like robbery," he said.

Weakly I waved him toward the telephone.

"You'd better report a homicide quick before the corpse walks out on you," I suggested.

He glowered, trundled over to the telephone, called headquarters, reported, and turned to us.

"You three stay down here while we look around," he ordered.

"Some one's coming," his sidekick said.

They made the porch as a gay young blade strolled up the steps lighting a cigarette. Tall, about twenty-two, slender, handsome, his hair was blond and curly, his face boyish and open— and surprised.

"Hello," he said, staring. "Something wrong here?"

"Who're you?" the big copper growled.

"I'm Hugh Jones. Live here. I say, what's happened?"

"Murder and robbery!" says the big flatfoot accusingly. He jerked his hand toward the open doorway.

YOUNG HUGH JONES saw the body, dropped the cigarette and paled. "My God! Is he dead?" He answered the question himself. "He is!" He moved into the hall, staring at the chair. "Poor old Smith," he muttered.

Nan Brewster reached his side with a little rush. "Hugh, where have you been?" Her hand touched his arm, I was the only one who saw the slight pressure of her fingers.

"I've been driving," he said, looking at her closely. "You're not hurt, are you, Nan?"

"No."

With a slight breath of relief he said, "Good." And looked again at the body. "I hope they get the man who did this," he muttered.

His composure was almost as good as Nan Brewster's. Young, both of them, but poised. Almost too poised. Perhaps Nan Brewster read my mind.

"I wish the ambulance would get here!" she burst out.

And we heard the jangling bell of the ambulance coming up the street.

They took the driver away. "Concussion of the brain," the interne told us. They were rolling down the drive when the homicide squad rushed up ahead of a couple of cars carrying reporters. The rush was on.

It was the same old story. Wise dicks, finger-prints, photographers, questions; the efficient coroner's man, prying reporters, and a growing crowd of curious onlookers gathering before the house.

Aunt Emma Jones held court in the drawing room with a bottle of smelling-salts in one hand and a grim, tragic expression on her face.

Nan Brewster was all wide-eyed innocence, so youthful, so appealing that those hard-boiled dicks and reporters fell over themselves with kindness and consideration. She tamed them, toyed with them—and at the finish they had nothing much from her.

Trixie Meehan got one aside to me. "She's a clever little devil, Mike." And then Trixie worked the same game on them.

Young Hugh Jones had not been there. They couldn't ask him much of anything. I was the goat. A man with a patch over a black eye had some explaining to do anyway. They raked me with questions fore and aft, made me repeat myself, tried to trap me, intimated I knew more than I did, and generally gave me a modified third degree.

The detective in charge was named Jorgan. He had a bulldog jaw, suspicious eyes and a skeptical manner.

"Listen!" I snarled at him finally, "If I'm under arrest, make a pinch! If I'm not, lay off. I've told you what I know. Jonathan Jones will vouch for me. I'm here to see him on business."

"Yeah?" Jorgan said nastily. "What kind of business?"

"Private."

"With a private gun under your arm, eh? There's a charge in that."

"Charge me and I'll beat it!" I snapped. "Where would I be if I hadn't had a gun when I walked in here?"

Jorgan shoved his jaw at me. "You better come down to headquarters and talk with us just the same," he said.

"Yah? I'll make you all sweat if I do. Come in the next room with me."

He went. I showed him my credentials. He batted his eyes.

"From the Blaine Agency?" he said. "Why didn't you say so? What are you doing here in town?"

"Jonathan Jones retained us. I want privacy. If the reporters smell me out, I'm useless."

"Okay. I'll cover for you," Jorgan said. His suspicious eyes searched my face. "I'll be looking for any dope you get on this, Harris."

"It's a deal," I agreed.

That let me out. One of the newspaper boys cornered me

on the front porch a few minutes later. He was sleepy eyed, medium sized, with carelessly combed hair and a round, plump, artless face.

"How come Jorgan laid off you so quick," he begged.

"We're brothers in the same lodge."

He grinned naively. "I'll bet you're kidding."

"Not a kid in a carload. Don't get in a lather about something that won't pay out," I advised.

"Thanks for the tip, Mr. Harris."

He wandered back in the house and I checked him as one man to watch. He was too artless, too naive.

The telephone at the back of the hall rang sharply as I followed him into the front hall. Hugh Jones answered it. He listened for a moment, and then spoke so loudly that everyone stared.

"Gone?" he almost shouted. "Kidnaped? Impossible! You're mistaken! He must be there somewhere!"

Jorgan leaped for the telephone. "Who's been kidnaped?" he rasped.

"Uncle John!"

Jorgan talked a moment and hung up.

"Jonathan Jones has just been kidnaped," he said curtly to the reporters crowding around him. "He was in bed asleep when the nurse last saw him. The window was left open."

7

THE DOUBLE SNATCH

IT WAS NEWS. The nearest reporter grabbed the telephone. The rest rushed out to their cars and drove furiously away.

In the drawing room Emma Jones had heard and fainted again. Hugh Jones was pale, excited. And for the first time Nan Brewster was knocked completely off her poise. Tears glistened in her eyes. She wasn't acting. She must have thought a lot of her uncle to take it this way.

I looked at Trixie. She looked at me. I strolled past her and said:

"Room 414, the Metropole. Tag the Brewster gal first."

I called a taxi, departed in it, got out down town and walked to the hotel.

The brunette at the cigar counter had closed up and gone home, which suited me. I went up to my room to wait for Trixie and examine the papers I had taken from that bouncing devil who had lurked inside Jones's front door.

I was getting groggy. This kidnaping was the final straw. It didn't make sense. If some one had tried to kill Jones by ramming his car, and wanted to finish the job, why hadn't they killed him off as he slept in the hospital bed? And my suspicions of Nan Brewster had been knocked into a cocked hat. She couldn't have been the one who had put Jones on the spot in his car. Not feeling the way she did about him. Or—could she?

I wondered, as I unlocked my door, if the papers in my pocket would give me a lead. I stepped in, snapped on the light—and shoved my hands in the air.

"Yeah! Now walk over here an' turn your back to me!"

He was leaning against the dresser, an automatic in his hand. Under the down-turned brim of his hat his eyes were staring coldly. His face was square and hard, and his voice was a familiar gruff rasp. I knew it instantly. He was one of the three who had mobbed me on that lonely country road. On the middle finger of his right hand was a big gold ring set with a triangular-shaped stone. My cheek had taken a print to match it. No doubt now this big bruiser was one of those who had half killed me.

I had murder in my heart as I walked toward him; walked right into the muzzle of that automatic with my hands in the air—and slapped it aside, hit him in the jaw with my other hand, and grabbed his coat.

He shot an instant too late. I'd done the impossible and he couldn't grasp it quick enough. No sane man would do what I did. Maybe I wasn't sane at the moment. That beating was too recent.

His shot drove powder sparks against my skin. The bullet burned my side and struck the metal end of the bed. And I had my automatic in his belly before he knew what it was all about.

"Drop it!" I bawled.

His rod hit the floor. His face went the color of old

dough. My side hurt. Smell of burnt wool and powder rolled up into my face as I showed my teeth.

"Where d'you want it? In your belly or in your head?" I asked.

Horror glinted in his eyes. He spoke like a sleepwalker, stuttering.

"D-don't! God, I ain't got a Chance!"

"I got a chance in that taxi, didn't I?" I raved, jamming the gun deeper in his middle. "Beat me up, will you? Try to run me out of town? You lousy country yegg! This is the payoff!"

He moaned. Yes, that big bruiser crawled. He couldn't take it.

"What's the idea of crashing the room?" I snarled.

He gagged, barely got it out in a whisper. "You d-didn't leave town. I w-was going to—to—"

I heard a sound at the window. Some one was outside on the fire escape. More of them, of course.

I almost shot him. Instead I knocked his chin up with my left fist and smashed him between the eyes with the gun. He squealed thickly, tried to raise his hands. I hit him across the temple as I dodged away from the dresser. I was facing the window in a crouch, gun ready, as he crumpled to the floor.

The curtain was up. Some one had been raising the window from the bottom. An indistinct figure was crouching out there on the fire escape. Again I almost shot with the automatic, but took a chance and held it.

"Come in or I'll let you have it!" I ordered loudly.

The man outside made no effort to escape. Pushing the window up, he stepped through painfully.

"Reach up and hold it while I frisk you!" I rapped at him.

Hands up obediently, he smiled slightly. Smiled without worry, as if there was an angle of amusement to it.

"If you're looking for a gun," he said, "I assure you I haven't one. I'd like to have one, in fact. That automatic on the floor will do."

That deep voice was familiar. So were those sunken, burning eyes. I wondered if I was dreaming or dizzy. I'd never seen his face before; but somehow I'd known it would look like this—gaunt, dark with the beat of fierce suns, cheekbones high, chin well defined. Not a pretty face, but strength in every line of it. Yes, strength; hard, implacable strength.

"How did you get here?" I said, looking at the patches of court plaster on his face. "You're supposed to be kidnaped. It's Jones, isn't it?"

He stood quietly, with a thin-lipped smile.

"YES, I'M JONES," he assented in that deep voice which was almost too large for his slender body. Quite casually he lowered his arms. I put the automatic back under my arm, still staggered by the sudden appearance of Jonathan Jones.

"I wondered what you were going to do," he said, nodding at the man on the floor. "He was in the room when I came up the fire escape. He had the light on until just before you arrived."

"You saw," I grunted. "How about you? When I left your room you were unconscious and smothered in bandages."

"Neat job, wasn't it," he smiled. "But deucedly uncomfortable. I made the doctor take them off when I came to. I had a slight concussion. It started to clear up rather quickly."

"Evidently. How about this kidnaping?"

He chuckled softly.

"I hoped that story would get out. There was no kidnaping. I dressed and left by the window alone."

"You could have walked out the front door."

"And everyone would have known it. I have important things to do. If I am supposed to be safely kidnaped they will be easier."

"D'you know your house has been robbed and your butler killed? Some one tore your study to pieces looking for something."

"Indeed?" he said, and smiled at some inward joke. But his face grew hard, bleak and cold right afterward. "I'm sorry about the butler. I hadn't counted on anything like that. I don't suppose you've done anything."

"Do? What'm I supposed to do?" I countered irritably. "I'm ordered here on a job and I walk blindly into a trap. Do you know this fellow on the floor?"

"Never saw him before. What kind of a trap did you walk into?" Jones asked.

I told him all that had happened. He sat down while I talked. He was weak and shaky, but his face was alert with interest. At the finish he said:

"They seem to know more than I gave them credit for."

"Who?"

"Don't know for sure," he mused; "But I'm afraid your life isn't worth much more than mine from now on."

"How much is that?"

He smiled slightly. "Very little. That's why I got in touch with the Blaine Agency. I need intelligent help."

I was glancing through the papers I had taken from that slender, dark man at Jones's house. The first one was a folded street map of the city. The second was a circular. I whistled as I opened it and found an advertisement for a well known sub-machine gun.

"This looks like business," I remarked, handing it to Jones.

The third was a letter postmarked in Singapore, addressed to Donald McDonald, General Delivery, Chicago, Illinois, U.S.A. The flowing writing was in a foreign language.

"Maybe this means something to you," I said, handing it to Jones. "Do you know a Donald McDonald?"

He grabbed for it, read it. His brows furrowed and his face became bleaker.

"I thought so," he said. "I know who's here now. One anyway. What's that?"

I was looking at the fourth item, a snapshot, broken at the corners, worn and stained from much handling. It was a white man, in a sun helmet, shorts, and puttees, with a cartridge belt and revolver around his waist and a rifle cradled in one arm. The face was lean, dark, hard. Four turbaned natives were standing in the background.

Across the bottom of it some one had written:

John Vanderman, Malay States, 1925.

I handed it to Jones without a word.

"I remember that," he said calmly. "It was snapped

up-country, above Selangor. I wonder how Hadji McDonald got it?"

"Who?"

"Sorry—Donald McDonald, the chap who received this
letter. He's a half-caste, Scotch father and a Malay mother.
Rotten break for him. They seldom turn out well."

"And John Vanderman?"

"Might as well let you in on it," Jonathan Jones said
slowly. "I haven't even told my family. I knocked all over
the East under the name of John Vanderman. Did a bit of
everything; made a lot of enemies and had a lot of fun. But
fever and hardship got me finally. I came home, assumed
my right name, took my place as head of the family and
the factory, which my younger brother had filled until he
died. I thought I'd left the past behind me."

Jonathan Jones gave me that mirthless smile.

"It seems we never leave the past very far behind. It's
caught up with me here. I'd more enemies than I thought.
A telephone call a few days ago gave me an inkling. It
spoke of something no one in America knew about—the
Golden Dragon of Yin Shee."

8

THE CHARM OF EVIL

CAN YOU TIE that? The Golden Dragon of Yin Shee? And he lays it under my nose as cool as a cucumber. "It sounds like a hophead's dream," I said.

"Yin Shee is a Chinese millionaire in Singapore." A big man. His Yin Shee Trading Company does a huge inter-island trading business. He owns ships, trading stores, plantations. On the side he runs guns and dope. Yin Shee's house flag is a golden dragon, flying on all his ships and marked on everything connected with him."

"A pretty story," I says.

"A prettier truth," he comes back quietly. "Yin Shee's dragon is a real golden dragon. It was kept with his ancestral tablets in Singapore. Been in the family for generations. Yin Shee was superstitious. That golden dragon was his source of power, prestige and success. He thought so anyway."

Jonathan Jones half-closed his eyes.

"Yin Shee betrayed me once," he said. "I struck back in the one way that would hurt him most—I took his golden dragon. And his luck turned at once. He went crazy. Offered fifty thousand pounds for its return, and ten thousand pounds more to anyone who killed me afterwards.

No pay for the man who killed me and failed to get the golden dragon."

Jonathan Jones laughed softly.

"A quarter of a million dollars for the return of Yin Shee's luck. Fifty thousand for my death. Every unscrupulous adventurer in the East went after that money. I missed capture, torture and death a dozen times before I cleared out."

The man became bright-eyed, vigorous, alive at the memory. I saw him for a few moments become John Vanderman, of the far places.

"How about the golden dragon?" I finally fired at him.

"Brought it back with me. It was too beautiful to lose, and every time I look at it I feel better about Yin Shee. He was a slimy Chink. He betrayed me and a girl I loved. She died. Yin Shee was to blame. I'm giving him a living death in return. He'll never amount to a damn any more. And while he's going down, he'll be thinking about me and eating his heart out."

John Vanderman was on his feet as he finished, face set in cold, furious satisfaction. For a moment we both were on the other side of the world in a welter of strange passions and adventure.

"You've got the golden dragon here in town?" I asked weakly.

"I have," he nodded. "I thought I'd dropped out of sight; but they've found me. One of my worst enemies, too. Hadji McDonald would kill me for his own pleasure. "But," said Jonathan Jones cheerfully, "he'll not do it until he gets Yin Shee's dragon. It's worth a quarter of a million to him. He's a practical man, from his father's side, I suppose. This letter is from Yin Shee, written in Dutch. He says money is sent and urges haste."

The gorilla on the floor stirred, groaned. His face was a mess.

"This mug was never in Singapore," I said.

He opened his eyes, groaned again. I grabbed him by the shoulders, heaved him to a sitting position. He whimpered. I put a shoe in his ribs to clear his head.

"Talk fast, you lug!" I says. "Who's in on this?" And I massaged the back of his head with the gun barrel.

He winced, cringed, put up his arms. I knocked them down with the gun. He whimpered again. I slapped his face.

"What's your moniker, sweetheart?"

"Manny Creeger," he mumbled.

"Where from?"

"Chi."

"Who's along? Who told you to tie a can on me?"

"I dunno," he sniffled, swiping at his bloody eyes with the back of his hand.

Grabbing a handful of his hair, I yanked back and shoved the rod against his lips.

"Spill it before I dig in your throat an' pry it out!"

He could go to town on a ride like that. And he went, blubbering like a baby, only a punk on the test.

"I dunno!" he bleats. "We got the office from a guy one of us met in Chi. He's laying big dough on the line to follow orders an' ask no never-mind. He's chippin' something damned substantial off the fellow who owns the local soap factory."

"Who met him in Chicago?"

"Stiffy Hawes. The other guy, Joe Reid, was here in town. He usta be in the beer racket in Chi."

"Your pals from Singapore got in quick with some of our best rats," I said to Jones.

And to Creeger, "Were you on that truck to-night?"

He denied it hastily. I lifted the gun.

Ducking against the foot of the bed, he moans:

"Hawes an' Reid done it! They got orders to have the truck at Beech Tree Drive an' Twenty-First in ten minutes an' smack a car that'd come out of Jones's place. I tagged in a taxi an' picked them up. That's all I know—s'help me, Mister!"

He seemed to be telling the truth.

"Where's the man who gave the order?"

He pushed the edge of his hand under his nose and swallowed hard. His eyes rolled in a hunted look, and dropped.

"I dunno," he said dully. "I been stayin' at the Elite Hotel with Hawes and' Reid. This guy telephones us. I ain't seen him since Chi. He's a little fellow, kinda dark."

I slammed him back to the floor. He lay there sniffling.

"A BIT ROUGH—BUT effective, eh?" Jonathan Jones said dryly. "Nothing like a little persuasion. I've used it myself. Do you think he can tell us any more?"

"He's only a mug. Handy with a gun and short on brains. Your man wouldn't let him know any more than was necessary. Does anyone in your family know about this?"

Jones shook his head. "They haven't even the vaguest idea."

"None of them would be interested in working against you? None would tip these men off that I was here in town and you were coming here to the hotel to see me?"

"I see what you mean," Jones tumbled quick. "That truck—and the taxi which waited for you at the hospital, eh? No, we can eliminate the family. Only my sister, my niece and the maid were there when you telephoned. The maid wasn't even near the telephone. You see it's impossible. They're my own blood. I had told them I was being threatened by a crank and to watch visitors and telephone calls. That was why you had trouble in getting me at the house this evening. But they would never let anyone know about it."

He had blind faith. I reserved judgment. Nan Brewster's covering for one of the three men who had murdered the butler was too recent. I'd seen queerer things happen.

"Okay," I says. "Now what? Did they get what they wanted at your house?"

He shook his head, grimly cheerful.

"They wasted their time, and killed my butler unnecessarily. I wasn't there. You've done good work, Harris. I was in the dark before. Now I know whom to look for and what to do. We'll get Hadji McDonald and whoever's with him—and the courts will dispose of them for murder."

"Just as easy as that," I grunts. "How so we do it?"

"They're in town."

"So are forty thousand others."

"That's your business," he comes back crisply. "I thought I hired a detective."

He had me there. From my bag I took a pair of handcuffs, dragged Creeger over to the radiator and handcuffed one wrist to the pipe.

"Work out of that, sweetheart," I says, "and I'll make you

Queen of the May. Let's go to the Elite Hotel and grab the other two," I tells Jones.

I'm thinking about Trixie Meehan as I say it, wondering what she's doing. If there was anything about Nan Brewster that would help us, Trixie would uncover it.

And just then the telephone rings sharply. I have a funny feeling that it's bad news as I grab the receiver.

"Hello," I says. "Who's...."

I never did finish. Trixie Meehan's voice came over the wire hurriedly, queer, tense, low, as if she was trying to speak without being overheard.

"Mike, they've got me! Trace this quick! The Brewster girl and her—"

Trixie gasped the last with a rush as a second voice cut her off. There was a jumble of sounds, and the wire went dead.

9

HOODLUM'S HOTEL

I JIGGLED THE hook, got operator. "What number was I talking to? What's the address?" I asked rather hurriedly.

"I can't tell you that," she says coolly.

"You'd better! It's police business!" I yelled.

"Hold the line and I'll check it," she tells me.

"What's the matter?" Jonathan Jones demanded at my elbow.

"Plenty!" I gave him cold turkey. "Your niece is mixed up in this some way—and the girl who's here in town with me has walked into trouble!"

"I didn't know you had anyone along," he gawped at me. "And as for Nan being—"

"Hold it!" I says. The operator was speaking. "The number you were connected with is Cleveland 3614. The telephone is listed under the name of R.B. Carstairs. The address is 1229 Dane Street."

Slamming the receiver on the hook, I swung on Jones.

"1229 Dane Street—R.B. Carstairs!" I threw at him. "That mean anything to you? Get that gun off the floor and come on!"

For a shaken, weakened man he got out in the hall after

me in record time; and as I jammed the elevator button he suddenly exclaimed:

"Slim Bob Carstairs! I wonder if it could be him!"

"Who's Slim Bob Carstairs?"

"A man," said Jones, "who is notorious from Bombay to Hongkong. An Englishman; a card shark, a ladies' man, a smooth devil. He's been blackballed from every club in the East."

The elevator dropped us down to the lobby and we hurried out front. I waved a taxi up, gave the Dane Street address to the driver. As we rolled off Jones said:

"Dane Street isn't a very savory neighborhood. What were you saying about Nan?"

"She's in on this some way." And I told him what I knew.

"There's some mistake," Jones insisted firmly. "You don't know the girl."

"I know what I've seen."

"Let it ride."

I rode the driver's neck for speed. I was in a lather about Trixie Meehan. She had a cool head, she always went out with a gun, she had been in enough tight places to wipe out all nine lives of an alley cat; but nevertheless she was a girl. She couldn't take all the odds and always come out on top.

Murder already had been done. It could happen again. A quarter of a million dollars—with fifty thousand thrown in for good measure—was big odds. I knew men who would kill for every hundred dollars slapped in their fists.

Dane Street was all that Jonathan Jones said it was. The street lights were far apart. Old brick and frame houses were dark with generations of soot, decaying into gaunt specters of the past. Most of the houses were dark. The sidewalks were deserted.

"A sweet place to hole up in," I said to Jones.

He had caught my tensity, and was fondling the automatic he had grabbed off the floor.

Stopping, the driver said doubtfully, "I guess that's the house. Too dark to see the number. Want me to look?"

"Never mind. Wait here."

I went to the porch, struck a match and read the number. "Next door," I said to Jones.

We cut across dry, bare ground where grass long ago had given up the struggle to exist. The next house was dark, too. Old brick, two stories high, it squatted under a heavy mansard roof in sullen decay and desolation. Our shoes scraped loudly on the cement porch.

The door was unlocked. I eeled in, gun ready for trouble. Nothing happened. I groped for a light switch, found it, and a dusty bulb overhead illuminated a squalid hall.

Jones's whisper grated on the silence: "The place seems deserted."

I didn't answer. His house had seemed deserted, also.

"Look at that," I said, and stepped across the hall and caught it off the floor—a woman's tiny black pump lying just inside the shabby living room.

That was all.

THE LIVING ROOM was deserted. A telephone stood on a table against the wall and a chair beside it had been overturned. Fresh tobacco smoke lingered among old, stale odors. An ash tray on a scarred center table was piled with cigarette ends. One cigarette had been dropped on the rug and left to scorch it. Jones picked it up, looked at the cork tip and lettering visible below.

"Curious," he frowned. "This is one of my brand. I'd have sworn I'm the only man in town who smokes these. I import them from England. Got used to them in the Crown colonies."

"Not so queer," I says. "This shoe belongs to Miss Meehan, the girl who telephoned me at the hotel. She didn't leave it there on the floor by mistake. She's smart. She knew she was leaving here and left her visiting card for me to find. This house is a dead cat as far as we're concerned."

I proved that in a few minutes by going from room to room, downstairs and upstairs. Not a soul was around. In a bedroom I found a suitcase plastered with the remnants of hotel and steamship labels. But it was empty. No clothes were around. The house didn't seem to be used much.

Jones was sweating now, too.

"I wonder if we hadn't better get the police," he suggested. "If Nan—"

"Take too much time. They can't do anything we can't. There's a murder rap floating around here. Your niece—"

"Nonsense!" he snapped. But he said nothing more about the police.

"Nothing around here," I said, heading for the front door. "Maybe we can pick up something at the Elite Hotel. It's been only a few minutes since that telephone call."

The Elite Hotel wasn't much better than the Dane Street neighborhood. On a side street, four stories high, its lobby was floored with badly worn linoleum and suggested a catch-all for poverty, resignation and lost hopes.

Four men were playing cards at one end of the lobby. Three more were writing letters. In one corner a woman was reading a newspaper. We drew little attention as we walked to the desk; and I judged that none of these late lobby sitters were on the lam from John Law.

"Are Mr. Reid or Mr. Hawes in?" I asked the clerk.

His collar was soiled, his face as pinched and furtive as the lobby over which he presided. He'd seen a lot of sordid life pass in front of his desk, I judged, and hadn't escaped all of it himself. Without batting an eye he looked at the key rack.

"Both their keys are out," he said. "Shall I call their rooms?"

"Never mind. We'll go up. They're expecting us."

Maybe he believed it; maybe he didn't. Jerking a thumb around the corner of the desk, he says: "The elevator's there. Top floor—407 and 409."

A dinge ran the elevator. His kinky hair was white and his creaky elevator cage was as old as he was. It crept up to the fourth floor; the door rattled back and we stepped into a wide, bare hall which had a narrow strip of ancient carpet down the center. Tin numbers were tacked on the doors. The wooden floor creaked out protestingly as I prowled along the corridor following up the numbers. The place was a dive, the kind that breeds trouble. I put my hand on the gun under my arm.

Jonathan Jones seemed to feel it, too. His face was hard, drawn. Flushed with effort. I guess the going was tough for him. He had worked a miracle getting out of the hospital; he must be drawing on his last reserve of strength now. But he kept on.

Rooms 407 and 409 were at the end of the hall on the right. The first door, 407, was standing ajar, the light burning inside. I shoved in, gun ready; and Jonathan Jones came after me.

A man was seated in a chair by the window, reading a newspaper. He brought it down with a startled movement as we stepped in and made a move to get out of the chair.

"Stay there!" I said in a low voice. "Where's your sidekick?"

Stocky, powerful, with a broad, flat face, darkening now in a scowl, he sat there looking into our guns.

"What's the idea of butting in here like this?" he asked.

He was calm enough about it. Too calm. But I didn't have time to think that over. There was a connecting door into the next room.

"Hold him," I says to Jones, and turned to the door. The flimsy walls would pass any alarming sounds. My hand was on the knob when a voice sneered behind me!

"Well, suckers, the heat's on you!"

10

A PAY OFF

OH, IT WAS a smart little play all right, as pretty a little
trap as I've ever walked into. He had followed us in from
the hall while we were paying no attention to the door. He
was standing by the bed, legs apart, holding a sub-machine
gun on us.

It was the same model I'd seen in the circular. And if
there's anything I hate, it's being on the noisy end of a
machine gun. I've seen men after they've been sieved by a
Tommy. An automatic or a revolver can miss if the move is
quick enough, but any man who gets funny with a machine
gun is rabbit meat before he starts.

I wasn't rabbit meat. One look over my shoulder, and I
dropped my gun like it was a hot potato and reached high.
Jones wasn't so quick.

"It's a sub-machine gun, isn't it?" he remarked, staring.
"I've never seen one before."

"And you never will again if you don't get those hands
up!" I yelped at him. "That guy's hopped up with dope and
feeling himself! Drop that gun!"

Jones obeyed.

The young fellow behind the gun wore a nasty grin. He
looked like a hoofer, dapper, with a jaunty soft hat turned

low in front. But he was a killer, drugged to the point of murder. It gleamed in his eyes, showed in the tautness of his body, the nervous shifting of his trigger-finger, the twitching of his face as he stood there grinning at us. He didn't even take offense at being called a dope. He was hopped up past caring.

"Maybe I'd better sew 'em up now, Joe?" he suggested—and I knew he was Stiffy Hawes, from Chicago. The stocky man in the chair was Joe Reid, the local boy home from the Chi beer days.

"Lay off that!" Reid snapped. "That older guy is Jones, the big soap boy. I don't know what he's doin' here, but it's all to the good."

He was on his feet, picking up our guns.

"Watch what you're doing, damn you!" he warned Hawes again. "None of your crazy tricks. I ain't going to take a rap because you get a rosy idea. One goofy move outa you an' you don't make no more, see?"

"Oh, yeah?" the hophead says softly.

His eyes flamed as he looked at Reid; flamed with murder. I thought for a minute he was ready to take his pal and us along with him. But he relaxed a little, and I breathed easier. It's no joke looking at a Tommy gun with a crazy lunatic fondling the trigger.

Some one knocked on the door.

The hophead jumped. I almost had heart failure as I saw his finger tighten spasmodically. Reid slid to the door, gun ready and an ugly expression on his face. A moment later he sang a different tune.

"Come on in, Maybelle! I figured it might be some one else. Thanks for that call from the lobby. We took 'em neat."

"Why'n hell didn't you walk in without knocking?" the hophead complains over his shoulder. "I almost set this typewriter off. My nerves are jumpy."

"Coking again, huh?" she retorted scornfully—and the brunette from the Metropole cigar counter walks into the room as cool as you please.

She had been the dame reading the paper in the corner of the lobby downstairs. She had spotted us and phoned up a warning while we rode the slow, rickety elevator. No wonder the reception had been hot.

"I see dice ain't all you're lucky with," I gave her sourly.

She gave me a lift of her lip.

"You just run into another revolving door, smarty," she says. "I hope Joe blacks your other eye."

And I saw the light. I had mentioned Jonathan Jones to her. The Metropole telephone desk was only a step from her counter. The telephone girl could have tipped her off about my calls; and she could have tipped her boy friends off. That still didn't clear up Jones's accident. He had left the house before she knew I was interested in him; but it was enough. I owed my black eye to her.

"They make a nice stylish cell for dames like you," I told her.

"You don't say?" she came back indifferently, and complained to Reid. "Do I get that party to-night, or don't I? I'm sick of taking the run-around."

"You don't!" says Reid emphatically. "And you like it. I got a job for you."

"I don't want no job. I got too much of a job now. My feet are killin' me an' I'm sick to my stomach from listening to wise-cracking Romeos all day."

"You can sit down on this one, sweetheart," he tells her. "You stay here an' hold a gun on these guys."

"I don't want to hold a gun on no guys."

"Shut up. I'm tellin' you to. We'll tie 'em."

Which they proceeded to do by tearing up a couple of sheets and binding our wrists and ankles. They shoved us on the bed.

"It could be better," Reid said, giving her my gun. "But you can hold 'em with this. And be careful of this guy Jones. He's worth plenty sugar."

"So this is Jones?" she said, looking at him with new interest. "He don't look so hot to me."

Jones wasn't looking at her. His glance had turned to me. We were both thinking the same thing. Jones wasn't worth a cent to any of them alive. But dead....

Those careless words had been Jones's death sentence. He knew it. A thin, wry smile touched his lips. Nerve there, all right.

REID HAD GONE into the next room. He came back carrying a worn leather bag which seemed to weigh a lot.

"We were getting ready to beat it when you telephoned up," he said to the brunette. "I don't know how long we'll be gone."

"Where you going?" she asked.

"It makes no never mind," the hophead chuckles. "Joe's going to open a safe."

"Joe! You're going to get into trouble!" she squawked.

"Nothin' to it, baby," says Joe. "The layout is all ready. They tell me it's an old-style box I can open with a coupla shots of soup."

"There won't be no trouble," the hophead says, and pats the blanket he has wrapped around the machine gun.

Reid gave him a dirty look.

"Let's get out of here before you open up on yourself," he grunts. "I never seen you ballooning around like this before."

They went out.

The brunette hefted the automatic like she had handled plenty of them before. A gun-moll from way back, that girl, hard as granite and cool as a snowbank.

"Well, boys," she says, "it looks like we're in for a lousy quiet evening. Anything I can do to make you more comfortable?"

"Take a dive out the window!" I cracks.

"Is that nice?" she says, leaning over the bed and tickling me in the ribs playfully with the end of my gun.

I snapped my feet in her middle and slammed her back against the opposite wall so hard the room shook. She squawked and the gun exploded.

I never knew what happened to the bullet. Springing on the mattress, I bounced over the side of the bed on my feet. They were tied tight, but I could still jump. I did, taking a long dive at her there against the wall. She squawked again as my shoulder hit her middle and we went down on the floor together. She squirmed a little and gasped and groaned, but that hard-boiled mamma was out of business for several minutes.

Jones was sitting on the edge of the bed as I struggled to my feet. With a hop-skip I kicked the gun away from her hand. Jones was struggling to free his wrists.

"Never mind that!" I snapped. "Sit on that female Capone, if she comes out of it!"

And I hopped over to the telephone, jarred the receiver off the hook, waited until I heard the clerk's voice in the receiver.

"Come up to 407 quick!" I called.

The brunette was showing signs of life. Jones sat on her, hard. She gurgled and lay there.

Jones was still sitting on her and I was waiting inside the door when the scrawny clerk looked in. His furtive face was a study in astonishment, alarm, uncertainty as he took us in. For an instant I thought he was going to bolt.

"Come in here and untie us if you don't want to ride to headquarters!" I grated.

That took him. He sidled in; and as he worked on the strips of sheet around my wrists he stammered:

"S-something wrong here? Some one telephoned down that a gun had been fired in one of the rooms."

He sniffed the air. The automatic was there on the floor. He knew something was wrong but he was too yellow to come straight out with it.

"Nothing wrong!" I snarled as my hands came free. "We're playing 'Tie-my-wrist-and-I'll-slap-yours.' Fix that other fellow!"

I freed my ankles and made for the telephone, getting my gun as I went.

"Anyone on the phone down there?" I asked him.

"Y-yes. The elevator man."

So I called police headquarters, asked for Detective Jorgan and got him.

"This is Harris, paying off from the Elite Hotel," I said.

"In room 407 there's a dame who can tell you something about the Jones case. She works at the Metropole cigar counter. The clerk's watching her. Come and get her."

I hung up before he could ask questions. "The police will be here in a few minutes," I said to the clerk. "Try and explain it if you let her get away."

She sat up and waved a hand feebly.

"You can't do this to me!" she bleats.

"It's done, sister, it's done," I told her. "And the next time you play being a wise mamma keep your stomach where it belongs."

Jones and I left them there. He grabbed my arm as we went along the hall.

"They went to open a safe!" he exclaimed.

"Uh-huh."

"And they know exactly where it is and what to do about it."

"Uh-huh."

We reached the elevator on that and I started it down.

"They had you figured for a corpse before they started. That means they went after the Yin Shee dragon, certain it was a cinch this time. You keep it in a safe, don't you?"

"Yes. But—but I can't see how they knew. They must have found it out since they left my house. How do they know about it so quickly?"

"Now I wonder how," I said, and let that ride. This was no time to be arguing with him about his family. "There's only one place you could have a safe at this time of night," I said. "The factory."

"That's where it is," Jones admitted. "What do you think we'd better do?"

"Go to the factory," I told him. "We're heading there now."

We stepped out in the lobby on that—and met the sleepy-eyed reporter with the round, plump face. He had been waiting there for us.

11

THE LUCK OF YIN SHEE

"SPILL IT, SWEETHEART," I said. "What's the idea of the gumshoeing?"

He looked as artless and naive as ever as he grinned at us.

"Am I surprised?" he says. "This is Mr. Jones, isn't it? Fancy running into you here while strolling around."

"Who is this man?" Jones asked me with a frown.

"He's a headache with a bright idea," I says.

"I just happened by," says the young man brightly. "But now that I'm here maybe you'd like to make a statement to the press, Mr. Jones. I'm Hal Deane, of the *News.* The report is out that you're kidnaped, you know. And," says brother Hal Deane, with an owlish look at me, "I hardly would call you kidnaped, since this gentleman was with me at the time the report was received at your home."

"And following up that bright idea about Detective Jorgan and me, you tailed me," I charged. "I'll bet you've been on me since I left Jones's house."

He grinned and did not deny it. Jones continued to frown. I sighed.

"I see you're a young man of action," I says. "How would you like to have a little more action?"

"Is there a story in it?"

"You'd be swept off your feet if you knew all that was in it," I told him. "Come along and see, since I know you'll be tagging from now on anyway."

"If you insist," he accepted meekly. "My car is outside."

So the lamb went to the slaughter with us. He looked slightly surprised when I told him to drive to the soap factory, and looked still more surprised when I made him stop a block away and we got out.

"I didn't think the factory was open at night," he said. "Uh—this is peculiar."

"You have no idea," says I nastily. "Is your insurance paid up?"

"I don't understand."

"You will," I promised. "Keep your mouth shut and your feet quiet."

Jones was leading the way along a dark street. We were on the outskirts of town. The old houses—shabby brick bungalows for the most part—showed no signs of life. The rank smell of the soap factory permeated the air. I never liked greasy smells.

It was hard to connect the dismal poverty about us with the romance of a shimmering golden dragon which carried the luck of Yin Shee, a Chinaman on the opposite side of the world. Strange things have happened to me, but none stranger than this—a millionaire leading the way toward men determined to kill him, an unsuspecting newspaper reporter tagging along, a crazy hophead fondling a machine gun somewhere in front. And I thought of Trixie Meehan and Nan Brewster, whom she had been watching, and wondered, half sick, if Trixie was still alive.

We reached the corner and the soap factory lay before us, to the left across a cobblestoned street.

It was a cluster of brick buildings surrounded by a high safety fence. Only the factory and vacant land lay beyond the street. Two spur tracks paralleled the street, passing through a gate into the factory grounds. On our side of them was a second traffic gate, with a watchman's shanty just inside. A dim bulb burned in front of that shanty, driving back the blackness around the gate. The factory windows showed dim lights here and there; but for the most part the big buildings loomed darkly, quietly, in the midnight hush.

A very prosaic, very drab, very peaceful setting. And yet the peaceful hush of the night made stark the isolation which lay beyond the cobblestoned street and about the factory grounds. A string of freight cars were spotted inside the fence, cutting off the lower view of part of the buildings.

We crossed the street toward the gate as silently as possible. Jones unconsciously lowered his voice as he spoke:

"We run only the day shifts now. Two watchmen are on duty at night; one at the gate around the yard and the other in the buildings. Everything seems right enough so far—just the same as it always is."

I had gandered all around as we started across the street. No automobiles were in sight. But I felt that old tightening of the nerves. Everything wasn't all right. It was in the air. The murky pool of light above the gate seemed crowded in on itself by the black shadows, which laced here and there along the ground like dark, waiting tentacles of some huge octopus.

"The watchman must be around the yard somewhere," Jones whispered as we came to the gate.

Yes, he whispered it; and Deane, the reporter, spoke uneasily under his breath:

"What's up?"

"Shut up," I told him; and he shut; and we passed through the gate in front of the little sooty watchman's shack.

The door was closed. It was peaceful enough—but as we went on I caught from the corner of my eye a faint gleam of metal at the side of the little building. Stepping over, I picked up a nickeled revolver which had been lying there. And, looking more carefully, I saw where the dusty ground in front of the shack had been smoothed—as if something had been dragged across it.

A moment later I was opening the shanty door.

THERE HE WAS—THE watchman—heaped on the floor inside, dusty and dirty where he had been dragged across the ground. No gun was in the leather holster at his side. He did not move. His bare head was wet on the side with fresh blood.

"Is he dead?" Jones spoke at the door, startled, husky.

And the chubby faced reporter craned in and said excitedly:

"Say, this is going to make a story after all!"

"Damn your story!" I told him curtly, closing the door behind me. I handed him the revolver. "Here, you'll probably need this. Make sure there's no dirt in the barrel."

"Need it?" he gawped. "W-what do you think will happen?"

"If I knew, I'd feel better. You stuck your nose in this and asked for it—now like it."

He was game enough, at that. He came along without argument. I had my gun in my hand by then. Jones had retrieved his from the dresser in the Elite Hotel where Reid had tossed it. He had it out, too. All three of us were armed, watchful—but it didn't make me feel any easier as I thought of the dapper Stiffy Hawes and that wild reckless look in his eye.

Ever try sneaking along a string of freight cars into blackness knowing that a hopped-up lunatic with a machine-gun might be lurking any place ahead of you with his finger tightening about the trigger?

Don't.

If I didn't sweat blood in the hundred yards or so we covered, I should have. I felt like it. We seemed to be grinding out loud noises with every step we made. I suppose we actually made no noise. But that machine gun....

Boooom....

Deane grabbed my arm. We stopped as the faint, dull concussion quivered on the night.

"What's that?" Deane whispered excitedly.

"Nitroglycerine, sweetheart," I breathed in his ear. "Leggo my arm before I clout you!"

He did.

"We turn to the right at the end of these cars and go over to the office," Jones whispered. "That's where the safe is, upstairs. They—they got it open, eh?"

"Maybe," I says, "and maybe not. That wasn't a big shot. He's probably going easy so he won't smash Yin Shee's dragon."

By now my eyes were used to the dark. When I stuck my head around the end of the freight cars and gandered over to the right I saw where the roadway we had been following crossed the tracks, passed the end of a big building and spread out into a large parking space before a smaller, two-story building.

A light was burning downstairs there. The upper floor was dark. Two automobiles were parked in front with their lights out.

"No cars should be there at this time of the night," Jones muttered in my ear.

He didn't have to tell me. Two cars. Hawes and Reid had come in one. And in the other?

"You two wait here for a few minutes," I said.

I kicked off my shoes and carried them in my hand as I cut out wide into the parking yard and came up behind the cars. Cinders, small stones, rough ground were brutal on the feet. But there was no light behind to silhouette me and in my bare feet I was more silent than the night itself.

Boooom....

A second faint explosion pulsed through the air I saw the faintest light flicker behind one of the upper windows. There Reid was evidently working with a flashlight in the reek of nitroglycerine fumes at his delicate task of blowing off a safe door without injuring the contents.

I wondered where the others were— and mostly where Stiffy Hawes was, with his machine gun.

He didn't seem to be in front of me. Only the two machines were there.

I was less than twenty feet away when, through the black glass of the left car, I saw some one move. The body creaked as weight was shifted. A man's voice spoke, murmuring something I could not understand. Then he chuckled in high good humor. And I knew everything was all right for the moment. I spread a little high good humor over my own face in the darkness as I slipped forward to the back of the car and to the side. What a surprise he was going to get!

I got it instead.

12

THE GUN ON THE STAIRS

ALMOST OVERHEAD A window was shoved up. The irritated voice of Joe Reid called: "Bring up that other flash from the back seat of my car." He was looking right down on me. It didn't seem possible he could miss seeing me as I froze against the rear fender.

The man who had chuckled put his head out the front car window a double arm's-length away.

"Righto," he replied. "Right up with it."

The window went down again.

He got out as I melted behind the car. He grumbled to some one else inside:

"The blighters should have carried a spare torch up there."

He turned his back to the car—and I knew this was the blowoff. There wasn't time to get out of the way. Putting my shoes on the ground, I crouched, waited. He stepped in front of me an instant later, tall and slender; and I hit him with the automatic quicker and harder than I've ever hit any man; hit him square on the jaw, steel against flesh and bone; and the dull crunch of the impact was not nice. You could feel—and hear—the bone breaking.

He ceased to exist as a danger. I took his weight full

on my shoulder as he started down, and eased him to the ground.

From the front seat another clipped British voice, slurred the faintest bit with a backing of accent, asked:

"Did you say something, Bob?"

Slim Bob Carstairs it was, who had been blackballed from every club in the Far East. He couldn't reply now; nor could I for him, with that clipped British accent to imitate. I grunted something, trying to think faster than I ever had before.

The other man must be Hadji McDonald, the deadly little Eurasian who had leaped at me inside Jones's front door. Undoubtedly he was armed. One shot, one bit of loud struggle, would bring a hornet's nest about my ears from upstairs.

I might get away from raking machine gun fire from an upper window. I might not. But I probably wouldn't be able to save Yin Shee's golden dragon. I wouldn't have any trace of Trixie Meehan. I wouldn't be much nearer breaking the case. They'd get away. Jones's life wouldn't be worth two hoots until they were caught again. It would be harder next time. They might use Trixie's life as a shield to hold us off. Yes, I thought of all that between two quick intakes of breath. I had to go on, kill or cure, sink or swim.

"Why the devil don't you answer?" He spoke again, louder. "What's the matter with you?"

I cleared my throat as I stepped around on the right side where Carstairs had been heading.

"I thought you had popped off for a moment," the little Eurasian grumbled from the front seat: "Better hurry with that torch. We can't spend all night here."

I could see him sitting inside the door. The window was down. His head turned toward me. I saw him start, heard his startled oath as he spotted my different build.

"Hold it, damn you!" I said through my teeth as I jumped to the door.

I think he went for his gun as he ducked back across the seat.

Before I could shoot a whirlwind erupted out of the back seat, caught him by the hair, yanked his head back hard over the top of the seat. He grunted with the pain of it.

Trixie Meehan said fiercely:

"No you don't! Get him, Mike!" Trixie had been sitting there in the back seat all the time. Her mind had clicked with its usual speed. I yanked open the door, slipped in, took a gun from his pocket.

"You *would* be lolling back here safe and sound while I've been in a lather about you," I grumbled at Trixie. "What have you been doing? Who's that back there?"

"Hmmph!" Trixie sniffed. "I see you are in a lather. It's the little Brewster flower. She followed her cousin and I followed her. He went in a house and she snooped under a window and I snooped after her and these two men caught us both and took us inside. This man—" Trixie yanked his hair—" left me alone near the telephone for a moment, and then caught me calling you. He dragged me away and slapped me."

Trixie yanked again so hard he groaned.

"The cousin didn't like it, but he couldn't stop us," Trixie said rapidly under her breath. "He was the third man I heard—that good-looking young Hugh Jones who came in while the police were there. He had been helping them against his uncle. They had involved him in murder. He was scared to death. No wonder Miss Brewster was covering up for him at the house! Her own cousin in on murder! She tells me she heard his voice and recognized it. She was stunned, thought of nothing but to keep it quiet; and then when he left she followed him to see what he was about. He guided them here. He's inside now. Where's the other man, Mike?"

"I cracked him down. He's back there."

Nan Brewster was crying softly as I grabbed the prisoner by the arm.

"Get out," I ordered, dragging him after me. He came silently. "You two lam for the gate—and keep going," I said. "Jonathan Jones and a reporter are over there by the freight cars. Tell 'em I'm going up in the office."

"Mike, not alone! I saw a man carry a machine gun in there!"

"I know."

"Mike!"

"Keep quiet" I said to Trixie. "I'm doing this and I can't stop to argue."

"What's he going to do?" weeps the Brewster gal.

And like the good little soldier she was, Trixie said: "Stop that sniffling, Angel Face. Don't you see what he's going to do—walk in there against a machine gun!"

I'll swear Trixie's voice broke a little at the last.

IT GAVE ME a glad little lift inside as I dragged my man over to the next car, made him get the flash and then marched him into the office and up the stairs. His cheekbone was laid open where I had hit him earlier in the evening. He was silent and vicious and waiting for a break.

And scared stiff, too. I think he knew why I was marching him ahead of me.

A man in front can stop a lot of bullets while you're ducking for safety. And maybe, if he's the right man, the bullets won't be fired.

But to Stiffy Hawes, wild with dope, no man was apt to be the right one.

I think Hadji McDonald, from Singapore, knew that, too, as he went up those stairs carrying the flashlight. Halfway up we passed a body on the steps. It had half a dozen bullet holes through the head. A revolver lay several steps below where it had been dropped.

I felt like a fool, I knew I was a fool, and I acted like a fool by going on past that. But I went, herding the Eurasian ahead of me. Just as we reached the top of the stairs a third, and heavier explosion, rocked the building.

He turned the flash on in the dark hall. His lagging steps were plainly audible as I steered him to the nearest door opening into the front offices. He went in first, the flashlight spearing ahead. The safe was at the left, at the end of the room, an old-fashioned box, out of date long ago. Outer and inner doors had been blown.

Hugh Jones was standing by the safe holding several lighted matches. The flashlight beam showed Reid standing beside him with a golden object in his hands. One glance was all I got, but it was enough to show the perfection of Yin Shee's golden dragon. All of eighteen inches long, perfectly modeled and proportioned, with open, bearded jaws, crested mane, lashing tail, it was exquisite and beautiful.

That much I saw—and then I forgot Reid, the handsome young man who stood by him, and the beautiful little dragon of gold. A lone figure standing at one of the front windows peering intently out, said sharply:

"There's somethin' out there!"

Stiffy Hawes started to raise the window.

More matches flared. The light reached me.

"That cop is in here! Get him!" Reid shouted suddenly.

Hawes swung from the window quicker than I thought possible. I snatched the flash from the Eurasian and spotted it on the window as the machine gun muzzle came around toward me. I knew Reid must be drawing his gun. Hadji McDonald had darted from my side. Nothing mattered but that gun muzzle swinging on me, with the two white hands gripping it tightly and the snarling face of Hawes behind it.

I shot twice. In the white light beam the hand on the front grip of his gun shattered, spurted red. I heard Stiffy Hawes scream with pain as the muzzle of the machine gun jerked back; and suddenly every other sound was drowned out by the tearing, hammering crescendo of shots. Fire licked in an intermittent stream from the muzzle as he dragged it around toward me again.

I shot twice more, snapped off the light, and dove to the floor; rolling clear over against the wall behind him before I stopped. The sleet of death cut through space where I had been standing—and abruptly stopped.

In ringing ears I heard him cursing, sobbing with pain and rage as he reeled about. Two more short bursts of fire raked the blackness. Bullets laced into the wall over me, bringing down a shower of plaster fragments.

"Joe!" he called.

Joe did not answer.

"Joe! Take this gun! He got me! God—I can't stand up! I'm spouting blood! *Joe!*"

He screamed the last—and Joe did not answer.

Downstairs three shots sounded in quick succession.

Stiffy Hawes collapsed an instant later. I heard the dull thud of his body, the clatter of the gun—and I came to my feet and snapped on the flashlight.

He rallied desperately on the floor when he saw the light. He tried to get the gun; and was still trying when I kicked it away. He reached under his coat, and I beat him to the holster and took an automatic. The madness was gone from his eyes now, and he was merely a gunman, dying.

I swung the light to the safe.

Joe Reid lay face down before the safe, where he had dropped from that first wild burst of machine gun fire. Hugh Jones, handsome and young and well bred, sat on the floor, his back against the wall, holding his stomach, gasping as he breathed. The blast of fire had caught him, too. But the slippery little Eurasian was not in the room, and the Golden Dragon of Yin Shee was nowhere in sight.

I rolled Reid over and looked in the safe. It was gone. Hadji McDonald had escaped and taken it with him. I was cursing as I ran to the stairs. Halfway down I met Jonathan Jones toiling doggedly up. He almost shot me before he saw who it was. He had used his last bit of strength and was on the point of collapse himself.

Deane, the reporter, was following, pale and shaky.

"Heard the machine gun—thought they had you," Jones panted, bracing himself against the wall.

"Not yet. But that Eurasian got away with the dragon. Did you see him go?"

Jones smiled—no, not soap manufacturer Jones—*John Vanderman* smiled at me, lifted the gun in his hand, and pointed down into the lighted hall with it.

"He didn't get away. I met him," John Vanderman said. "Yin Shee has lost his luck again."

The little Eurasian was on the floor just inside the door. His hands were reaching out, and just beyond them, where it had fallen right side up, the Golden Dragon of Yin Shee was facing him.

That broke the case.

I called the police, ambulances, yelled for Trixie and with her gave first aid. They took Jonathan Jones back to the hospital again, but not before he shook my hand, and smiled, and said:

"The Blaine people sent a good man. I'll call them next time I need help."

And as they took him away I said bitterly to Trixie:

"I hope he stays out of trouble until I get my vacation. I'm heading for Times Square on the first train."

Trixie Meehan put her little hands on her little hips and looked me up and down.

"You should!" she said. "And I'm going with you to see that you get there. You're too dumb for a small town, Mike Harris. Any man who hasn't got sense enough to stay away from a machine gun needs a guardian."

"But not you, baby," I gave her. "That tongue of yours gets in my hair. I wouldn't be caught on the same train with you."

"Yes?" says Trixie sweetly. "Watch!"

So we went back to Times Square together.

MURDER HARBOR

*It Was a Spectre Ship, Steered by a Dead
Man's Hand—Why Did It Follow Mike
Harris Down That River of Vanished Men?*

1

MISSING!

THE TRAIN PUT me in New York on one of those cool, bracing mornings you sometimes get in late summer. The kind that makes you feel it's a good world to live in. I felt that way as I taxied to my apartment, changed, read my mail, and went on to the Blaine Agency.

I was just in from Ohio, where I'd cleaned up a queer case at a soap factory and almost got my head shot off. I was going to turn in my report and get that long promised vacation. Sweet leisure. I felt so good I tipped the hacker half a dollar.

And then, sitting in Thompson's office, I found Trixie Meehan, cool as a cucumber.

"Hello, Ape," says Trixie brightly. "I see you got here."

Trixie had been on the Ohio case with me. We had started back together; as usual we had wound up in a fight and ridden opposite ends of the train. I hadn't seen Trixie in the station. I didn't want to see her now. I pitched my hat on Thompson's desk and growled:

"I knew something was going to spoil my day. Where's Thompson?"

"Out," says Trixie. "All set for your vacation, Mike?"

"Nothing'll stop it this time!"

My foot smashed hard on his hand,
Jamming it against the gun.

I wondered about the odd little smile on Trixie's face.

Maybe you've never heard of the Blaine Agency. Or me—Mike Harris. Or Trixie Meehan, the smartest little woman operative who ever pulled a rod on a crook. Little, pert, with a baby doll face, all innocence, Trixie had a sharpshooter's mind, and more action than any four other pint-sized females. I always gave her that, no matter how she got in my hair.

Just then Thompson came in hurriedly. Thompson was all dick, and a good one. He ate, slept, breathed nothing but Blaine Agency business. As Eastern manager he demanded results, without excuses. Thompson started talking as soon as he hit the office.

"I'm glad you're both here. I just called your apartment, Mike. I need you."

A head and shoulders poked up from the ladder.

"What'd'you mean, *need?*" I came back. "I'm on my vacation today."

"I know," says Thompson placatingly, as he dropped in his chair and laid the chewed stub of his cigar on the desk edge. "You've got that vacation coming, Mike. A nice long one. You've been doing fine work and you're entitled to a rest. You know, Mike, you're one of the best men we have. I was telling Mr. Blaine himself the other day that when Mike Harris gets on a job it's as good as sewed up."

I took it fishy. When Thompson finished handing out lilies there was usually something sour in the air.

"Let's have it," I said.

Thompson had the grace to look sheepish. He picked

up his cigar stub, chewed the frayed end a moment, put it on the desk once more.

"It's this way, Mike. You'll have to put off that vacation a few days— Sorry," he said hastily, as I gagged. "Orders from the old man personally. I've just been in to see him."

"Nuts to the Old Man!" I yelled. "Whose vacation is this? I've worked like a truck horse for years. Every time I get my fingers on a vacation someone plants a heel on them. I'm heading for the country now. I'm going to lie under a tree and forget crime, crooks, and the whole damn Blaine organization. And fresh female dicks!" I added for Trixie's benefit.

Trixie smiled demurely.

"Now, Mike, was that nice?" she asks. "I was sitting here feeling sorry for you when you came in. Mr. Thompson's secretary told me there was a job for you."

That explained her dirty smirk.

Thompson heaved a lugubrious sigh.

"You know I'd do anything in the world for you, Mike. I'm going to Mr. Blaine himself and tell him you've got to have a vacation. You've earned it. It's coming to you. Take plenty of time off and have a good time."

"Now you're talking. I knew you'd come through for me."

"You bet I will," says Thompson, from the heart. "I'll see that you get it—after this one little job is cleaned up."

Trixie snickered.

Thompson looked like a sorrowful father.

And once more my vacation spread wings and flapped neatly away. No use arguing. I was on the spot and I might as well take it.

"What's the dope?" I demanded, wearily.

THOMPSON BEAMED.

"I knew you'd come through, Mike. This is an urgent case. Very important. The party concerned is a personal friend of Mr. Blaine. You may have heard of him. Mathew W. Bronson."

"Never did. He's only a pain to me."

"Mathew Bronson is the president of the Bronson Steamship and Navigation Company. The Bronson Line."

"What did he do, rob his safe?"

"Disappeared."

I shrugged. "Let the cops find him. He's probably sneaked off for a vacation himself."

"That's out."

"Then he's kidnaped. Wire the Department of Justice."

"He's been gone thirty-six hours and there has been no demand for ransom."

"Amnesia. Women trouble. Money troubles," I guessed. "It ought to be easy to find him."

Trixie said demurely: "Then it should be easy for you too, Mike."

"Keep out of this!" I snarled at her. "Whose vacation is ditched, yours or mine?"

"Now, now," Thompson soothed. "I'm putting you both on this case. Here's the layout. And it's one of the most important you've ever had—for the old man's personally waiting for reports.

"Night before last," Thompson said, "Mathew Bronson worked in his office until seven o'clock. Then, with Eldridge, the vice-president of the company, he went to the Bronson pier to inspect their new ship, the Crenona. She's a passenger ship, due to sail for Mediterranean ports at noon today. Bronson and Eldridge dined aboard. Afterwards they inspected the ship thoroughly. At about ten-thirty, while Eldridge was having a last few words with the captain, Mathew Bronson walked down the gangway and disappeared."

"Just stepped off into thin air, I suppose?" I cracked sarcastically. "With men all about the pier and a watchman on duty at the entrance?"

"That's what makes it all the more peculiar," Thompson nodded. "Bronson's limousine and chauffeur were waiting just inside the pier entrance. The Crenona was taking on cargo. The place was swarming with longshoremen. No one even noticed Bronson come off the ship. The watchman at the pier entrance swears he didn't leave that way. The chauffeur didn't see him. Inquiries made a few minutes later found no one who had noticed Bronson. The gangway watch saw Bronson start ashore, but something drew the watchman's attention just then and he didn't see Bronson step off the gangway."

"In other words, maybe Bronson never got off the gangway?"

"Exactly."

"Maybe he jumped in the river and called it a day?"

Trixie said sweetly: "He wouldn't have done that, Mike, because he's only been married a few weeks to a beautiful young woman. I saw it in the papers at the time. He had everything to live for."

"If he was married to any woman, he probably was ready to jump in the river," I gave Trixie sourly; and to Thompson: "Where do we come in on this? It's a straight case for the police."

Thompson struck a match, puffed his cigar alight, took it from his mouth and let it begin to smolder out again.

"It isn't," he said. "The police aren't wanted on this. No publicity is desired. In fact it's very important there be no publicity."

"Have it your own way," I shrugged.

"Furthermore," says Thompson, "Mathew Bronson has to be found in the next two days. Either his body or his person must be accounted for."

It sounded silly to me. "Why?" I asked.

Thompson shrugged. "I'm giving you orders that were handed to me. The rest is up to you two."

I yowled, "Are you kidding me? The man walks off his ship and disappears. No clues. No reason for it. Forty-eight hours to find him. I'm no Houdini! I can't pull a shipowner out of a hat like a rabbit!"

Thompson set his jaw. By that sign I knew he had been stepped on pretty hard from above.

"You'd better," Thompson told me.

2

A CLEW

TRIXIE AND I left the building together. Outside, I looked at her.

"Forty-eight hours!" I snorted. "The thing sounds screwy to me. Why don't they want publicity?"

"I'm sure I wouldn't know, darling," Trixie said with false helplessness.

"Find out then! Go up to Bronson's apartment and ask some questions of that sweet mamma. I'll take the steamship pier and his office. I'll get in touch with you through Thompson or his secretary."

So Trixie went one way and I went the other. A taxi shot me downtown to the Bronson pier on the lower west side. I made it between eleven and twelve and landed smack in the middle of the pre-sailing rush. The last cargo was going over the side. Passengers, luggage, friends were underfoot, coming, going over the gangway. A natty young officer at the foot of the gangway gave me a cold eye when I asked:

"Where can I find the watchman who was on duty at the head of the gangway night before last?"

"No visitors for the crew right now. They're all busy," he said.

"I'm representing the company."

"Uh—I see. 'Fraid you'll have to identify yourself. Mr. Eldridge, the vice-president, is standing over there. If you'll have him okay you."

He pointed to a man standing some twenty feet away, watching the preparations with a bored air. I went to him.

"I'm from the Blaine Agency," I told him. "Investigating Mathew Bronson's disappearance. I want to speak to the watchman who was at the gangway when Bronson left."

Eldridge was a tall, stooped man in his early forties. A brown suit which needed pressing hung loosely on him. His face was thin, cheek bones prominent, chin squarish. Nothing particularly outstanding about his face—until I looked through rimless eyeglasses into his chilly gray eyes. Then I knew why Eldridge was the vice-president of the Bronson Steamship and Navigation Company.

Those chilly gray eyes were uncompromising, ruthless. Eldridge was a power, no matter how he appeared at first glance.

He said levelly, "Why do you wish to see the watchman?"

"I want to know exactly what happened."

"I can give it to you. I talked to the man."

"Tell me later. I understand Bronson must be located within forty-eight hours."

Eldridge stared down at me. I'm red-headed, short, not much bigger than Trixie Meehan; Eldridge topped me by a good head. His cold eyes studied me, took me apart, made a decision.

"Just as you like," he agreed indifferently. "I'll get the man for you. This way, please."

He took me aboard to the captain's quarters, warning

me on the way, "No one here knows that Mr. Bronson has disappeared. Don't mention it."

Eldridge knocked on the captain's door and, when the captain appeared, said curtly: "Get the watchman who was on duty at the gangway the night I went ashore."

And the captain, stocky, grim, imposing, says as meek as you please: "Yes, Mr. Eldridge." And hurries off to obey.

Even captains, it seemed, did not always run things. Eldridge stood there without expression, eying me.

"You people move fast," he said abruptly. "You were only notified about two hours ago. What are you going to do?"

"Ask questions," I replied.

"How many men are assigned to this case?"

"Can't say."

It was no use telling him that a mob of dicks running around in circles would only confuse things. As fast as Trixie and I turned up leads, men would be assigned to run them down.

"Whom are you going to question?" Eldridge pressed.

And I said, "The watchman—you—anyone who was on the pier at the time Bronson disappeared."

Eldridge smiled faintly. "A thorough young man, I see. Call on me for anything I can do. I'm greatly worried about Bronson."

"Why wasn't this case turned in sooner?" I asked him.

Eldridge pursed his lips. "We thought Bronson might have known what he was doing. He's that way, rather secretive, strong willed; does things at times which don't seem logical."

"Mmmmmm. How old is he?" I asked.

"Fifty-one."

"And his new wife?"

"Twenty-five." Eldridge gave me a long look from his chilly eyes. "What do you know about her?"

And I grinned. "Nothing. I understand they haven't been married long."

His cold eyes bored at me. I'd have bet my next pay check to an old corn plaster we were both thinking the same thing. A man over fifty had no business getting romantic with a girl twenty-five.

THE CAPTAIN RETURNED with a weather beaten seaman wearing a white duck uniform.

"Here's the man, Mr. Eldridge," he stated.

I said: "I'll talk to him alone, over here by the rail." And I led the man there.

"Remember night before last, when you were on duty at the gangway?" I asked him.

He had looked worried; now he appeared relieved.

"Sure, I remember it," he nodded. "I ought to. I've been asked enough about it. Say, what's wrong? They've asked me so many questions I can't figure it."

"Mr. Bronson lost something that night. We're trying to trace it."

Hastily he denied, "I didn't see him lose anything."

"Who said you did? You saw Bronson start ashore, didn't you?"

"Sure—I did that. I was at the gangway when he started ashore. I see him halfway down an' then looked away. That's all I know."

Nothing shifty about his looks or manners. He seemed to be telling the truth.

"Pretty busy on the dock, weren't they?" I asked.

"Plenty. We were taking on cargo. Lights. Lots of noise; you know how it is when they're rushing cargo."

"I know. Now, listen—think hard—before Bronson left the ship, or after you last saw him, did you notice anything out of the ordinary?"

His forehead scrunched into deep wrinkles of thought.

"I didn't see anything," he denied. "His chauffeur was waiting at the foot of the gangway for him."

I hadn't heard this before.

"How d'you know it was his chauffeur?" I fired at the seaman.

"He came up the gangway an' ast me when Mr. Bronson would be ready to leave."

"And what did you say?"

"I said I didn't know."

"Who else have you told about the chauffeur?"

"Nobody."

"Why?"

"Nobody ast me," the fellow said stolidly.

"When did you last see the chauffeur?"

"He was standin' down there when Bronson started ashore."

The seaman shifted a hunk of tobacco into the opposite cheek and looked blank and patient. Getting facts from him was like pulling pin feathers from an old rooster. Eldridge, I saw, was still talking to the captain, paying no attention to us there by the rail.

"When you looked again, Bronson was gone? And the chauffeur was gone, too?" I said.

"That's how it was."

"What did the chauffeur look like?"

"Kind of short and dark. Had on a dark uniform an' cap, an' black leather leggin's." The seaman stopped, shifted his tobacco again, added: "An' black gloves. I noticed 'em on account of the weather being warm. Gloves looked funny."

"He might have had wooden hands," I cracked—and that dumb seaman took me seriously, shook his head. "His hands looked all right as far as I could see. He used 'em coming up the gangway."

"Skip it. Was this chauffeur the only stranger you saw? The only man who asked for Bronson?"

"Yep."

"Okay," I said, and turned away.

ELDRIDGE LEFT THE captain and joined me. "You found nothing, I suppose?"

"What does Bronson's chauffeur look like?" I came back.

Eldridge shrugged.

"Just a chauffeur," he said. "Rather thin. He was waiting in Bronson's car just inside the pier entrance—but he saw nothing of Bronson. I've already questioned him."

"Is he short, dark-skinned?"

"On the contrary—a lanky Scotchman named McDonald." Eldridge half drooped his long eyelids. "That's a queer question to ask," he suggested slowly.

"I'm that way—queer. Why must Bronson be found dead or alive within forty-eight hours?"

"Business," Eldridge replied shortly. "We must have information about him in that time."

I let it go. "Did Bronson have any business worries, any money troubles or woman tangles?"

Eldridge shrugged. "Not that I know of."

But the man's manner suggested that he was holding

something back. I knew that at the moment there wasn't much chance of getting anything out of him if he didn't want to talk. But I tried once.

"Had Bronson received threats of any kind?"

"I'm not aware of any. He probably would have told me," Eldridge declared firmly.

We walked down the gangway on that. I looked around.

"I think I'd like to question some of the stevedores who were working around here at that time," I decided.

"It has already been done. None of them noticed Mr. Bronson."

"I'll want the address of the pier watchman who was on duty at the entrance."

"We can get that at the pier office," said Eldridge; and we did so quickly at his command.

Henry Regan, on West Eleventh, was the name and address.

"Anything more?" Eldridge asked me pleasantly. "Regan will tell you just what he told me, I'm sure. He saw nothing of Bronson after we went aboard the Crenona."

"I'll talk to him just the same," I decided.

For a moment I thought Eldridge was going along with me, but he didn't. On West Eleventh I found Henry Regan on the point of going to bed. Big, cheerful, he had old carpet slippers on his feet and suspenders hanging down around his trousers.

"Sure, I was on duty night before last," Regan said. "I see Mr. Bronson's car go in. Checked it like I do all trucks and automobiles."

"What did the chauffeur do?"

Regan pushed a hand through thinning hair.

"Nothing much," he said. "The driver talked to me some an' sat in the car some, an' when I asked him if he didn't get tired waiting, he said he was used to it. We got into an argument about Scotch whisky an' Irish whisky. He's a Scotchman with a burr that'd take the skin off your ears. We was still at it when Mr. Eldridge came to the car an' asked where Mr. Bronson was."

"How long had you two been arguing about whisky?" I asked.

Regan scratched his ear reflectively. "A good half hour it was," he guessed.

I LET HIM go to bed, got Bronson's number out of the telephone book and taxied to the upper Park Avenue apartment house.

I was feeling pretty good by then, despite being dragged off my vacation. I'd struck a faint lead and I wanted more of it. A tricky French maid admitted me to the swanky Park Avenue apartment and I met the young woman Bronson had married.

The man had taste anyway. She was a knockout. Tall, slender, perfectly poised; but now she looked worried, had evidently not slept much the night before. She spoke nervously.

"A young woman representing the Blaine Agency just left. Have you found out anything about my husband yet?"

"We're making progress, Mrs. Bronson."

Her face lighted with relief.

"What is it? Please tell me," she begged.

"Later," I said, "When I know more. I came here to ask your chauffeur a few questions."

She was dressed for the street. She said: "I was just going out. McDonald should have the car at the curb now."

We went down together. As we crossed the sidewalk, a big blue limousine moved up in front of us. The chauffeur who jumped out was bandylegged, freckled. He wore a gray whipcord uniform.

Mrs. Bronson said: "McDonald, this gentleman wishes, to ask you some questions. He is from a detective agency."

McDonald looked at me expectantly. I let him have it.

"I just wanted to know," I said, "why you went on board the Crenona to ask when Mr. Bronson would be leaving?"

He wrinkled his forehead, looked at Mrs. Bronson, at me, shook his head.

"I dinna go on the Crenona, or ask questions a' any mon on 'er," he denied.

"The gangwatch said you did."

McDonald's jaw shoved out at me.

"He lied, beggin' your pardon, ma'am. I wasn't away from me car except to talk to the pier watchman. He was only a step away."

"Must be a mistake then," I said. "Sorry. I wouldn't worry too much if I were you, Mrs. Bronson. We're pushing this."

I left them there, walked a block, hailed a taxi, and rode back to Eleventh Street, and routed Regan out of bed. He didn't like it but he had to take it.

"What other automobiles were on the pier that night?" I asked him.

"None!" he denied grumpily. "The Crenona wasn't taking passengers yet an' there wasn't any other ships at the pier.

Some of the ship's officers came in taxicabs—but they walked in."

"What about the short man in the dark chauffeur's uniform who went on the pier that evening? He looked like an Italian, didn't he?"

"He did not," Regan denied flatly. "Because no man like that went on the pier. I'd remember him if he did. Chauffeurs without cars ain't got no business on the pier after dark. I'd have made him account for himself."

"Sure about it?"

"Listen, that's my job!"

So I let Regan go back to bed and walked over to the Bronson pier on the track of an idea.

No one paid any attention to me as I prowled about, going clear to the end of the pier, looking down at the black piling rising out of the restless green water.

Mathew Bronson had walked off the Crenona and vanished. A chauffeur had been waiting for him. Not his own chauffeur. The man hadn't been seen entering the pier, or leaving it.

A kid could have gotten the answer.

If Bronson didn't go ashore, he left by the river. A growing hunch whispered that along the waterfront I'd get my first news of the man.

And I did.

3

THE SIN DOCTOR

I KNEW THE waterfront from many prowlings, sometimes disguised, sometimes as myself. I prowled it now as Mike Harris, dropping a careless question here and there. Finally I wound up with the Sin Doctor.

Maybe you've never heard of the Sin Doctor. Along the waterfront, the bleak stretches of the Bowery, the canyons, alleys and dark hideaways on the lower end of the island everyone knew him.

Tall, erect, always wearing a neat faded black suit and an old drooping black felt hat perched on a bushy shock of white hair, the Sin Doctor had a regular beat.

Before repeal you'd find him in the dives, the "smoke" joints, flop houses, pool rooms and grimy little speakeasies. The Sin Doctor never worked, never begged, and yet he always had a spare coin for a down-and-outer.

Now and then you'd see him talking quietly to some derelict. More than one man and woman had changed the course of their lives after talking with the Sin Doctor.

But for me the Sin Doctor was a walking dictionary of everything that went on along the water front. I found him in Jake's Place, just up from Battery Park. I bought a beer, drank it slowly, caught the Sin Doctor's eye—and he followed me out into the street. We walked down the block under a sky that was looking more like rain every minute.

"I have not seen you for some time, Harris," the Sin Doctor said in flawless English. "Am I wrong in suspecting there is something on your mind?"

I slipped him a grin. This tall old man was wise. He'd seen about every form of vice and sin there was; and he spent his life looking into the minds of men and women.

"I need help quick," I told him. "Haven't got time to root around and turn up any leads. I've got to find out if someone along the waterfront here kidnaped a man night before last. Got him as he was coming off the Crenona of the Bronson Line. And if they did, where they took him and why. I've got to find out if he's alive or dead."

The Sin Doctor looked at me. His face was long, thin, kindly, marked with lines of suffering and wisdom. I never knew what had sent him to the water front, but it was marked there for any man to see.

"You know I don't talk," he said quietly.

"I know," I admitted. "A cop couldn't pry a secret out of you with a crowbar. But listen—this mustn't get out—Mathew Bronson, the steamship owner, has vanished. I've got a hunch he was snatched off the Bronson pier. His young wife is pretty hard hit over it. For some reason the police can't be notified. He's got to be found inside of forty-eight hours. It's up to me."

I didn't remind the Sin Doctor of past favors rendered him and further ones waiting. I didn't have to. He'd helped me out before; me alone, Mike Harris, and a woman in trouble would get him. It did.

"I haven't heard a word about Mathew Bronson," he said

reflectively. "But last night I overheard some one say a man named Gimpy Lewis must have made a killing for he had a new fast speed launch."

"I don't know him."

The Sin Doctor sighed.

"Gimpy Lewis," he said, "is a scrawny young man, worthless and beyond hope of redemption. He takes drugs and for the last year or so has been a member of the Hugger gang of dock thieves. They have not prospered lately. Some of them have gone to prison. Yet last night I saw two men who I know to be connected with them spending money freely. I have heard of no big water front thefts which might have provided it."

A thin spat of rain began to fall as we talked. We stepped under an awning.

I knew about the Hugger gang. Wharf thieves, booze runners, hijackers, they were an institution along the waterfront. They took murder, robbery and arson in their strides. But they had never really been in the big money; hard times, inability to buy protection had hit them hard.

The tip sounded hot.

"Where can I find this Gimpy Lewis and the other two?" I asked.

The Sin Doctor looked out into the rain, then at me.

"Gimpy Lewis had the launch tied at the third dock down from the old green Morgan Line Pier. Number 49. He undoubtedly uses the same place most of the time he is on this side of the river. I believe he stays quite a bit over on the Jersey side. It is not well policed."

I knew that too. Parts of the Jersey waterfront were almost wilderness, deserted, decaying from disuse.

"Anything more you can tell me?" I begged.

The Sin Doctor shook his head.

"I'm afraid not. The launch is green. I will send you word if I hear of anything more, Michael."

AN EMPTY TAXI came along. I left the Sin Doctor there under the awning, waved the taxi down, told the driver to take me to Pier 49. There in front of the old green pier warehouse I turned up the collar of my coat and walked through the drizzle to the spot where the green launch had been moored.

It was there, half hidden under the piling, rocking to the slow swell. Just beyond it, a high stack of lumber had been piled on the dock edge. Behind that I waited. The slow drizzle, the chill it brought were nasty.

I thought about my vacation; about Thompson, comfortable in his dry office, and said things under my breath. But I waited. The green launch moving restlessly below me was the only tangible clue I had to follow.

Not much of a clue either; merely a hoodlum who had blossomed out with unexpected prosperity. But if the Sin Doctor thought it worth investigating, I did too.

I waited an hour. The drizzle slackened; but the bleak afternoon grew bleaker, fading under the gray, low hanging clouds.

They came—unexpectedly, three men walking on the dock planking, talking. Hoodlum talk, hard, sure, certain.

"Jeeze, Jack, you're yellah! Hell, I'm tellin' you the thing's a cinch. You got a good boat. We can use you."

Jack growled back, irritated. "Who's yellah? You guys are nuts. The thing's hot!"

The third man spoke, sneering.

"Sure it's hot! What the hell? Think we'd be layin' a cut on the line if it wasn't? It's so damn hot somebody could burn plenty if it don't go through. Do you take a piece or don't you? Are you yellah or ain't you?"

"Who says I'm yellah? I'll see you on it. What's the lay?"

They stopped beyond the lumber, by a rickety wooden ladder leading down to the launch. Shoes scraped as one started down. The first who had spoken said:

"Now you're talkin' sense. Your boat's right, ain't it?"

"Yeah. You oughta know that?"

"We need it, Jack. I ain't so sure about this new one yet. She's fast, but maybe she won't hold up. If the coppers from the Battery get on our tail, we need plenty on the eight ball. We'll meet you about nine tonight off Pier H, on the Jersey side. Have it—"

The rest faded out as the speaker went down the ladder.

Behind the lumber I felt good. It sounded hot. The Sin Doctor had come through with a bang. And then the wind tripped me up—one of those nasty, hard little gusts which come off the bay when you least expect it. My hat sailed out from behind that stack of lumber, tumbling over and over in plain view.

4

CORNERED!

SILENCE FOR A moment—then a startled oath rang out.

"What tha hell! Hey! Somebody's behind that stack of lumber!" And from the launch—" Grab 'im! Here's my rod!"

A gun hit the dock planking—but I was already on my way. Three against one jacked the ante too high. I had no gun. I dove out from behind the lumber as the gun bounced and the man standing there grabbed for it.

He was a hood all right, short, powerful, with a bullet head and long arms. A bad customer. Apt to shoot first and ask questions afterwards. And he'd have my back for a target if I ran. I swerved at him.

He saw me from the corner of his eye as he grabbed for the gun. He was taller, heavier—but it didn't do him much good as my foot smashed hard on his hand, jamming it against the gun.

How that hood yelled! He staggered, grabbing for me with his other hand as I jolted into him, jammed his head down with both hands, bracing myself while I slammed a knee up hard.

It got him full in the face. The shock went clear to my hip. And that hood's second yell dropped off in his throat.

He reeled dizzily—and I shoved him toward the edge of the dock. Stumbling, staggering, he tried to keep from going over as a head and shoulders poked up from the ladder.

The fingers I had tramped on still held the automatic. No time to get it. I turned, raced for the shore end of the dock.

Ever run from a bullet? It's hell. I could feel that lead slapping into my back every step. In half a dozen seconds I lived years. My feet seemed on a treadmill, getting nowhere.

Then the shot crashed.

I ducked, dodged. It didn't help, of course. Only hasty aim saved me that time. Maybe my dodging did help a little in the next few steps—as two more shots blasted the damp quiet of that old pier.

"Get the so-an'-so."

No need to wonder if that yell meant business as I dodged to the right through a two foot door opening and raced through the cavernous pier shed. I heard them coming. And I ran. How I ran—bursting out into the semi-security of West Street, that wide trafficway which parallels the dock front.

Automobiles, horse drawn drays, pedestrians, were in sight. More than one head was staring as I traveled fast across the street. Half a block away a copper started toward me.

I still expected a bullet to catch me between the shoulders. But none came. When I looked over my shoulder they hadn't even followed me out into West Street.

Panting, I stopped. It had been a close call. One bullet placed right—and I'd have gone into the cold green water before I finished kicking on the dock planking. Ever have that weak feeling in your knees? Mike Harris, of the Blaine Agency, had it right there in the open when he stopped.

I WAS LIGHTING a cigarette when the cop lumbered up and grabbed me.

"What's the idea?" he puffed. "What'd you run across the street for?"

He was young, big, husky. Indignant now. And he didn't get any better when I drew deep on the cigarette and grinned at him.

"Officer," I said, "believe it or not, I was doing my daily half mile. Doc's orders."

He scowled down at me, gripping my arm tighter.

"Don't hand me a line like that!" he snarled. "I seen you taking it on the lam out of there. I heard shots. Come clean before I rough you."

I laughed at him. It wasn't good judgment; but this young copper's bluster was a far cry from that cold crawling feeling down the middle of my back.

"Officer," I says, "you're doing your duty like a man. But don't rough me out here in the street. I'll have your shield and a big pan in the papers for bullying an innocent citizen. It won't do any good to wave the commissioner under your nose—but if you want the truth, I was standing out there on the pier when three hoodlums made a dive for me. I ran. They cut loose with a gun. Write your own ticket on that."

He continued to scowl suspiciously.

"Sounds damn screwy to me," he said.

"I'll bet," I agreed. "Now listen, what are you? A copper or a grand-stander? Do I get a break or do you make a play to the audience? What about those men who shot at me?

Look them up—and let go my arm. I run to you for help—and you arrest me. Will that read nice?"

They were swarming toward us, half a dozen, a dozen, coming to see what all the fuss was about. My braw young copper gandered at them, gave me another scowl and let go my arm.

"Show me those three guys," he ordered, and started across the street, drawing his gun.

I went along, enjoying my cigarette. I'd delayed him long enough. It doesn't make sense? Be your wisdom! Of course I didn't want the copper tangling with them. He might have made an arrest, and then what about Mathew Bronson? I had a sure fire lead. Their shots missed me. No hard feelings—and tonight on the Jersey side of the river was my ace in the deck.

The copper shoved in ahead of me and peered through the semi-gloom of the dock shed.

"No one in here!" he snapped.

"Outside, officer—through the door there. I was halfway down the pier by a pile of lumber."

He gave me a dirty look, edged through the door and looked.

"Are you handing me a pipe dream?" he snarled. "There's no one out here!"

And there wasn't. Not even the sound of the launch motor. I looked over the side. It was gone. I grinned.

"Officer," says I, "now will you believe there's a Santa Claus? I told you I was taking my daily dozen. Maybe you just thought you heard those shots."

That wrecked him. He didn't know whether to crown me or argue.

"I heard 'em!" he said. "There's something screwy about all this!"

"I'm not the screwy one," I sighed. "And I'm not packing a gun. What are you going to do about it?"

He was all copper, and he played his hand out in a copper way.

"Come on," he says, grabbing my arm. "We'll search this pier and if there's nobody here I'm going to run you in for investigation."

He could have run me in for anything. I didn't even argue as he searched the pier and drew a blank.

The copper searched me and didn't find a gun. He was fit to tie by then.

"I'm going to run you in!" he raved. "And I hope they give you life. I think you're lying and I don't like your face. Red-headed mugs like you take away my appetite."

"Officer, you slay me. Next time I go out I'll wear my hair to suit you. Let's get over to the precinct station and let them see what a dumbbell you are. But don't call the wagon or I'll take it clear up to the commissioner. I'll buy a taxi."

So we went around to the precinct station; and a couple of wise dicks got hard as they fired questions at me; and I called Thompson; and Thompson called where it would do the most good; and the precinct got sat on from the throne room; and they turned me out like a hot potato that was burning their fingers.

I was still laughing as I rode uptown to the Blaine Agency office.

5

PURSUIT

THOMPSON SAID, "YOU'RE a hell of a detective. I send you out to hunt a man and you get yourself arrested."

"That just goes to show," I said, "what a good man can do when he puts his mind to it. I want a fast motor boat. One that will outrun anything in the harbor. And I want the exhaust silent and a searchlight on the bow."

Thompson canted his cigar up toward one eye and looked me over.

"Anything else you want?" he demanded. "Maybe you'd like an elephant, and a pair of dancing teddy bears to make you happy?"

Trixie Meehan, seated against the wall, crossed one leg daintily over the other and looked scornfully at me.

"Poor dear," she cooed. "He can't take it. He's getting hysterical."

"But I can get it, lady," says I to Trixie. "What did you dig out of Bronson's wife?"

"Nothing much," replied Trixie calmly. "She's a smart wench."

I thought of that tall, poised young woman. "Wench?"

"You heard me. Wench!"

"That woman's a lady worried to death about her husband."

"And your grandfather probably had red hair on his bald head," Trixie retorted. "If she's worried about Bronson I'll go into an old ladies' home and knit socks."

"Yair? Didn't I talk to her? Didn't I see it?"

"Mike," said Trixie wearily, "you don't know anything more about women than other men. Poor dears, you all think you're wizards. Bronson married a two-timing hussy."

Trixie took a cigarette from her pocketbook, looked at Thompson and me scornfully.

Thompson cleared his throat.

"Umm—this is the first time I've heard of this," he said. "Er—a—interesting."

I didn't give her an argument. When little Trixie Meehan laid it on the line like this she had the goods. I coaxed:

"Come on, sugar, spill it. How come the hussy and the two-timing?"

Trixie yawned behind the soft fingers.

"When I went to the door of Bronson's apartment, his wife was just finishing a telephone conversation inside. The last words she said were: 'I'll watch it, darling, and I'll be there in an hour!'"

Thompson said: "Hmmmmmm—"

Trixie had a wicked glint in her eye.

"I guess she watched you, Mike. Made a convert out of you, didn't she?"

I snorted. "Who's 'darling'? Some gigolo?"

"Darling," said Trixie calmly, "could probably buy gigolos by the dozen. I was sitting in a taxi down the street when you walked out with the lady, grinning like a tomcat at her.

When she got rid of you I followed her. She drove to Times Square, dismissed her car and taxied to upper Riverside Drive. She walked a block further and went in a big house."

"Why," said I, "all the secrecy?"

"Her darling seems to be a man named H.C. Eldridge. At least he lives in that house."

You could have spread my limp jaw on a slice of bread.

"Eldridge?" I bleated.

"Exactly," Trixie agreed smugly. "Vice-president of the Bronson Steamship Company."

Thompson almost swallowed his cigar.

"The devil's teeth!" he got out past it "Are you sure about that?"

"Did it rain this afternoon?" Trixie countered, and answered for herself. "It did. I was in it. I got damp waiting for those two love birds to leave the brick nest. A taxi collected her finally. She went back to her apartment. And," said Trixie, "I came here. Now what?"

"Put a man on Eldridge. See where he goes, and what he does."

Thompson cleared his throat.

"That's already been done. Miss Meehan telephoned in and I sent a man to Riverside Drive. So far he has not reported back."

There we were. The case was broadening out. Getting hot. It would be boiling if this kept on.

"Better put a couple of men on Eldridge and a couple on Bronson's wife. Check every move they make. And do I get that boat?"

"He still wants a toy," Trixie murmured.

Thompson surveyed me through half closed eyes.

"You get it," he said. "Why?"

I told him.

Thompson looked doubtful.

"Not much to go on there, Mike. It's only a hunch."

Trixie went to bat for me like she always did in a pinch.

"Mike's hunches usually work out. He knows what he's about if you want this cleared up, you'd better play ball with him."

"I am, I am," Thompson assented hastily.

I GOT MY boat; got it at a quarter of eight that evening in the small boat anchorage down by the Battery.

A man named Bartlett owned it—a young chap—society type. God knows what strings Thompson had pulled; I didn't ask Bartlett any questions as we stood on the landing stage and looked down at the speed boat.

It was a beauty—long, slim, fast. All white paint, mahogany and brass. A brass trimmed searchlight was mounted on the covered deck forward of the control seat. Bartlett cradled a high powered sporting rifle in his left elbow. He was about thirty, tall, tanned, athletic. A cheerful chap with the collar of a sport sweater turned up around his neck and a white yachting cap cocked over one eye.

"Think it'll do?" he asked with a grin.

"It ought to," I said, turning my coat collar up against the cold fog swirling around us.

Yes, there was fog, brought on by the change of weather. It was the last thing I wanted, but I had to take it.

"Let's push off," I said.

Bartlett cast off, stepped down behind the steering wheel; and in a few minutes we were plowing out into the river. Sleek, powerful, alive, that speedboat cut into the harbor swells. The underwater exhaust was a mere purr behind us. Bartlett tossed a light kapok life jacket on my lap.

"Slip it on. No telling what will happen."

He was right; anything might happen in this fog. I put the jacket on under my coat.

"Think you can find your way?" I asked.

"Blindfolded to any spot in the harbor," Bartlett replied cheerfully.

He was getting a kick out of this. I think if he had known what was coming he would still have gotten the same kick.

About us the harbor pulsed with life, even at this time of evening. Half smothered, the deep-toned bellow of a freighter's fog horn sounded somewhere off the bow. Bartlett sheered slightly off on another course. He turned on the searchlight. The brilliant beam stabbed through swirling fog wraiths and was quickly blotted out.

"*Whoooooooo....*"

That was another whistle, far off down the harbor, stealing through the thick blanket like a mournful cry. The gray fog smothered everything. My face felt as if a wet towel had been slapped across it.

Bartlett steered that launch with the hand of a master. Now and then he stopped the engine; we drifted while he listened to the vague muffled noises. Finally he stopped the motor for a long time; said: "There's the Chambers Street ferry ahead. We'll edge in to shore and drift down to Pier H."

Running the motor in spurts, drifting some, we edged through the fog.

A thin piercing whistle drifted over the river. Bartlett chuckled.

"That's the Sadie Bowers. Captain Joshua Bowers. He's a character. No other whistle in the bay like it."

Then, from the shore side—the muffled rhythm of a gasoline engine exhaust. Close. Coming closer....

I felt Bartlett lean forward, trying to place the sound. In the thick soup it might have come from almost any direction. Always closer. Bartlett switched the searchlight on, swung it right, left, swearing softly as the beam lost itself in the gray, drifting mist.

And that exhaust came closer—closer....

"Look out!" I shouted.

Bartlett spun the wheel, started the motor. But we both knew it was too late. We braced ourselves....

Out of the fog, a slim boat length away, into our misty searchlight beam rushed the bow of another launch. A launch without lights, running recklessly. I caught one glimpse of the white curling' bow wave; then as our boat moved sluggishly—

Crash!

6

DEATH IN THE FOG

THE IMPACT THREW us together. Our boat heeled far over, shipping water. Wood ground, splintered, as the launch which had rammed us pushed on, swinging us around, tearing at the splintered side.

"Shut off your engine, you damn fool!" Bartlett bawled to the other craft as he came to his feet.

He was ignored. Our launch swung around, grinding alongside the other craft.

Swearing, Bartlett hauled the searchlight around on our splintered side. The hole torn there was widening as the sharp prow ground in it and began to slip out. Water poured in.

Despite the kapok life jacket I had a sickish feeling as I looked at the black heaving water alongside. Cold, that water—and the current would sweep us down into the wide lower bay.

No sound came from the other craft, no hail, no movement as it swung free, began to forge ahead.

"Jump on it!" Bartlett yelled.

We scrambled from our reeling, stricken craft into the other and were borne off into the fog. We were in an old, open cockpit type launch with the motor housed at the back.

Groping forward, I touched the back of a man sitting at the steering wheel. Grabbing him, I yelled:

"What's the idea of running us down?"

The shoulder swayed—toppled—fell—tumbling heavily, inertly against my legs. And still the man made no sound.

And the launch pushed aimlessly into the fog.

Over the limp body I felt for the controls, found the ignition, cut it. The motor died; the launch coasted, water slapping against the bow in diminishing crescendo as headway died. And I dropped to a knee, striking matches.

The stranger lay there, twisted half double on the damp, floorboards, face down. His head was bare; his hair black, sleek, shiny. He was short; he wore a dark chauffeur's uniform—and I knew I was looking at the man who had met Bronson at the Crenona's gangway. Knew it even more definitely when I hauled on a shoulder and turned up a thin face with a distinct Latin cast.

Over my shoulder Bartlett uttered: "For God's sake— what's that?"

The matches burned out. Three more flared—and I turned the limp figure over and saw what my hand had felt. The side of the shirt and coat were damp with blood. Fresh blood, wet, gruesome.

"My God!" Bartlett exclaimed.

In the man's back was the bullet hole, small where it had entered; larger in his breast where it had come out after tearing through the heart. This wild, free running launch which had crashed into us had been piloted by a dead man.

Our drift had stopped entirely now. The launch rocked

gently. The fog seemed to press down, thick, ghoulish, with its damp breath over this spot of death. Stealing through it came the hoarse bellow of distant whistles. Off there was life—and here in the silent fog with us—death.

Mechanically I wiped a blood-smudged hand against my trousers leg and asked myself what the dead man was doing here in the launch. Who had killed him? How far had the fast running launch come with its grisly burden?

Bartlett was wondering too. He said: "It was angling out from shore. Hard to tell where it came from."

I struck more matches, searched the bottom of the boat. No gun there.

"Wasn't suicide," I said. "And I doubt if anyone else was in the boat." The words were hollow, unreal in the stillness.

The staccato blur of another fast running engine came pulsing through the fog. It stopped... started up again. Listening, we heard the invisible craft circling somewhere nearby. Stopping... going on again.

"It's looking for something," Bartlett said under his breath. "Let me at that wheel. I forgot my rifle. Got a gun?" He sounded anxious, concerned.

"I've got an automatic."

Bartlett started the motor. The old launch gathered speed slowly, shaking with the propeller drive which rolled water at the stern. And suddenly, unexpectedly, the hammering beat of the other exhaust was all about us. A shaft of light came swinging through the fog, swept over us, swung back and bathed us in a sickly glow. Boiling through the fog another boat sheered for us.

Bartlett and I ducked as the thin crack of a gunshot came simultaneously with the vicious scream of a bullet.

"Damn them!" Bartlett raged as he crouched in the bottom. "What's the idea?"

"Probably only in fun," I yelled as a second bullet made us duck lower.

The searchlight held full upon us in a halo of misty light. Looking back I saw a tiny finger of red light flash out. Another bullet screamed past within a foot of my head.

No one could know Bartlett and I were in the launch. It was a dead man who was being attacked. More shots came, some missing us by inches, some smacking into the wooden hull with sharp, dead impacts. Bartlett crouched by the wheel, spun it hard. The launch slued off, slipped out of the light into the gray dark fog.

THE SEARCHLIGHT GROPED vainly as the other craft swerved too late. The light dimmed out, vanished. The boat rocked as Bartlett scrambled to his feet and changed course sharply again. Motor wide open, we cut back across the other craft's wake.

Once I caught the dim weaving glow trying to locate us. It vanished. Bartlett got his bearings in some mysterious fashion and bore downstream.

"We didn't get the fish we were after," he said cheerfully.

"Hard to tell what we got."

"We can heave him in the river," Bartlett said. "Probably as good as he deserves. I don't like his looks."

"Nix. Nothing like that. He's got to be carried in and reported. That means an investigation. Maybe they'll hold us."

I was on my knees as I spoke, searching through the dead man's pockets. They were empty; not even a hand-kerchief; nothing at all to show who he was. By flickering match light I looked for tailor's labels and found that they had been ripped out.

From the front of the boat Bartlett spoke cheerfully. Nothing seemed to faze him.

"We can take him to the Harbor Precinct Station at Pier A. I know Captain Evans there. He'll be reasonable."

"If we get there," I said. "This boat is taking water."

"Bullets through the hull below the water line," Bartlett guessed. "Pier A it is then—and we'll hope."

Pier A it was, down to the tip of the island and in alongside the lighted float in the basin, under the stern of a police boat moored here. Two huskies with police caps on their heads looked down at us without interest.

"Ahoy!" I called.

"Yup—what is it?"

"We've got a dead man here for you."

"Yair? Toss him back in before he bites you. This is too dirty a night to be picking up floaters."

"Come down here and get him before you go to sleep against the rail," I gave the big ox. "Who said this was a floater? He hasn't been in the water yet. He was shot while running this boat. Where's Captain Evans?"

They tumbled away from the rail while Bartlett stepped out on the float. I was following him when I glimpsed something white in the dead man's clenched left fist. In the flickering match light and the excitement I had overlooked it before.

The fingers were tight, as if in death they had sought to hold, hide the damp, crumpled visiting card I pulled from them. One look at the lettering: Miss Patsy Ryan, Haddon

Arms—and I thrust the card into my pocket as the two men off the patrol boat came running along the float.

"What happened?" the first one called.

From the float I jerked a thumb back at the body.

"Ask him," I said, and followed Bartlett into the station house. Captain Evans was at a desk in a back room—a stocky, square-shouldered man with a grim, weatherbeaten face.

He greeted us with gruff cordiality. "Hello—out late tonight, aren't you? Don't you amateur sailors ever go to bed?"

Bartlett chuckled.

"It's the fog, Captain. Can't resist it—or handle it with the old dash either. We were rammed by a launch out in the river. Sank our boat. We tumbled into the one that hit us and found a dead man. He'd been shot through the heart. In case you'd like to look at him, he's out there by the float."

Captain Evans stood up, staring.

"Rammed by a launch with a dead man in it?"

Bartlett nodded easily. "Out in mid-channel. I can't get the answer. You'll have to unwangle it."

"This," Captain Evans snorted, "makes a dirty night perfect. Let's have a look at him."

Half a dozen members of the harbor patrol were on the float when we got there. The body lay at their feet. Captain Evans took one look and snorted again:

"Running a boat and wearing a chauffeur's uniform! What the devil did he think he was doing? Hacking in the harbor?"

"Something for you to figure out, Captain," I murmured.

He hunched his shoulders, looked us over carefully.

"Just what were you two doing out in the harbor tonight?" he demanded.

"Taking the air," Bartlett grinned at him.

Captain Evans grunted, fired questions at us; and when he was through he knew no more than when he had started. Neither Bartlett nor I mentioned the third boat or the Jersey shore in which we had been interested.

"Queer. Doesn't make sense," Captain Evans stated, scowling doubtfully. "Come in the station and put it down on paper."

Fifteen minutes covered that—and Bartlett and I walked out of the station and left them the dead man and the launch.

"Now what?" Bartlett asked me.

"Seems to be all—and thanks for the buggy ride. The Blaine Agency will make good your launch, I guess."

Bartlett shrugged the idea away, as if one launch more or less did not matter.

"Anything more I can do?" he questioned. "I don't know what this is all about, but it's corking so far."

I had to tell him: "No more tonight. I'm going this way. Hope to see you again."

I cut across Battery Park with that visiting card burning a hole in my pocket. It hadn't been there in the dead man's hand by accident. There was a reason. Had to be a reason—and I was going to find it.

7

A LEAD

THE HADDON ARMS was on the fringe of Greenwich Village, a four-story walkup, neat but old. Miss Patsy Ryan's name was on the mail box for apartment 202. I walked up without announcing myself and used the door knocker.

The door opened half a foot. A cautious glance inspected me. She wasn't cordial. Not that lady with her short, snappy: "What do you want?"

"Miss Ryan?"

"Maybe. What is it?" She was chewing gum. Behind the edge of the door her jaw never stopped moving while she kept a suspicious eye on me.

"Who did you give this to?" I asked, flashing the damp visiting card.

She was a cool one, with the list of answers.

"Most anyone," she said, looking at the card. "Where'd you get it?"

"In a dead man's hand."

"Oh, yeah? I should pass out my cards to dead men. Use a better line than that, mister, on your way out."

She started to close the door. My foot stopped it.

"Maybe you'd like to know more about the dead man," I

said, handing it to her in a lump. "He wore a dark chauffeur's uniform and I'll bet he's no stranger around Little Italy. Good-looking young fellow—until he started riding on the river and they put a bullet in his back. He had this card of yours in his hand when he died."

She'd have fallen or toppled if the door hadn't been there to hang on to. Her fingers went bloodless as they gripped the edge, and her face went bloodless too; that pretty, rather sullen face with the brightly rouged lips.

"Dead?" she uttered thinly.

The door swayed in. I thought she was going to faint before I could get in and catch her. She clung to my arm as I kicked the door shut; clung, trembling, with black burning eyes searching my face. A shudder ran through her. She drew a deep breath. Her hands tightened.

"Dead?" she repeated. "*No!* It can't be! Not dead! You're lying! Damn you, you're lying!"

Her sharp, tinted nails dug into my arm as she shook me.

"You're lying!" she panted.

And I couldn't even grin with the satisfaction of knowing I'd hit a bull's eye. This grief was too real, too sharp and devastating to draw a grin.

"Sorry," I said. "It's true. Who was he?"

Her eyes were glassy. Her look at me became fixed. The last drop of blood receded from her face.

"Dead!" she whispered—and went out this time like a wind snuffed candle flame.

I got her before she hit the floor and carried her across the living room to a couch. Then I scratched an ear and wondered how long her faints were good for. Maybe there was time to search the apartment and get a line on her before she came out of it.

A picture on the mantel caught my eye. From a gold frame a familiar young man looked at me, sleek black hair and all; only in the picture he wore a well-tailored suit and rated nearer a second-rate gigolo than the chauffeur we had turned over to the detail at Pier A. Writing scrawled in the lower corner of the picture said:

"To the end, Tony."

I was thinking he had probably never visualized the end this night had brought, when I heard the door open quickly and softly behind me; and I swung around to meet a curt, sharp, hard order.

"Lift 'em, guy! Hoist 'em!"

WHEN THEY TALK like that behind my back I never argue. I lifted 'em as I completed the turn and got an eyeful of a bad sight.

He stood there with his right hand down in his coat pocket and a gun muzzle outlined plainly through the cloth. Without taking his eyes off me he reached back with his left hand and closed the door.

"What's the idea?" he asked. "Who the hell are you?"

He could make it sound bad. He looked bad. Red-faced, raw looking, like a hunk of meat snatched off a butcher's block, his jaw had a bulldog thrust, his mouth was narrow, tight and mean; and above it the nose was short and flattened. He looked ugly, he sounded ugly, and as far as I was concerned he was ugly.

A shrug was the best I could give him at the moment.

"Just a friend," I replied, and hoped it sounded as easy as I wanted it to. He had come loaded for trouble. "I dropped in and—er—Miss Ryan has had a weak spell. You'd better help me with her."

His right ear was thickened at the edge. Wrestling, I guessed. He was built like a wrestler, all solid muscle and bone; and the corners of his mouth went up in a canine quirk as he sneered at me.

"Sure, I'll help her," he said. "Get back there against the wall beside the couch."

He pulled the gun out of his pocket—a revolver—and waved me to the wall; and when I was there he walked to the couch and roughed her face hard with the palm of his left hand.

It must have hurt, but it worked. She shuddered, opened her eyes, rolled them wildly for a moment, and then sat up with a gasp.

"Get up!" he growled at her.

She did so without shrinking; she knew him, paid little attention to him even when he asked roughly: "Where's Tony?"

But she wasn't having any of it. She was still dizzy from the jolt I'd given her. Hands clasped, she began to sway, moaning: *"He's dead! He's dead! He's dead!…"*

He slid a nasty look at me, rasped at her: "What d'you mean, dead? Who's dead?"

"Tony! They shot him! Killed him! Oh, my God, I can't stand it!"

He caught her arm, shook it. "Lay off that! How d'you know he's dead?"

"He—he told me!"

She pushed an accusing finger at me; and the roughneck glared at me and shoved out his big jaw.

"Who is this guy?" he demanded.

"I d-don't know! He c-came here about Tony!"

Sobbing, she walked blindly across the room. He ignored her. His narrowed eyes bored at me.

"So!" he said. "You were one of the guys in that boat with him?"

It was a statement, not a question. The hunch of his head and shoulders was ugly, threatening.

"What boat?" I says, without batting an eye.

But he had the answer pat.

"Damn you!" he snarled. "Don't stand there and lie to me! I'll put a bullet through your belly if you don't come clean!"

"What'll that get you?"

I wasn't as big as I sounded. Nothing like the business end of a gun to cut you down. I'd looked in plenty of them—and never failed to get weak in the knees waiting for the crash, the shock of the bullet.

This fellow meant business, but he'd probably shoot me quicker after I talked than before.

He had another answer pat, with a nasty grin as he moved toward me.

"Maybe it won't get me anything. But I know what will. I'll beat your ears in with this gun barrel an' see how you can take that."

I'd been trying to figure how to get at my own gun before he could drop me—and I couldn't. There might be an outside chance as he raised the revolver; but an outside chance, no more.

I dropped the idea suddenly, took a step back to stall

him, keeping my face blank. He couldn't see what I was watching.

She had walked blindly across the room, that sobbing girl; still sobbing, she had stopped before a bureau and opened a drawer without noise. She took out an automatic and turned, swiping at her wet eyes with the back of her hand. He didn't know she was coming toward him with a haunted, desperate look on her face.

But I did; and I waited, hardly looking at her. For her eyes were on him, not me.

"When I'm through with you, your own mother won't know that map!" he grated. "Come on—do you talk or don't you?"

I could grin at him then. I did.

"You're going to get an awful surprise," I told him.

"*Yeah?*"

He got it the next moment.

8

MURDER HOUSE

SHE SHOVED A full inch of the automatic in his back; for a moment Mike Harris wasn't in the picture.

"What tha hell?" he bawled with the shock and pain of it as he staggered forward.

"Give it to me!" she sobbed shrilly. "I'll k-kill you if you don't give it t-to me!"

And she would. I saw it on her face, murderous hysteria which would shoot if he hesitated an instant. He didn't ask her what she wanted. Without a word he put the gun up by his shoulder where she could reach it.

She snatched it, backed off with a gun in each hand, still sobbing as she threatened: "If you turn around I'll sh-shoot!"

Never had that mug been nearer the pearly gates than he was then. Tense, rigid, he stood waiting. I could see his shoulders cringe as he waited for the shock of the bullet.

She backed to the door, opened it, stepped out, closed it and was gone.

He heard the door click and was across the room after her as I drew my gun.

"Heist 'em, you mug!" I yelled.

His hand was on the doorknob when he looked over his

shoulder. He took a chance, snatching open the door and diving outside.

He was a big fish. I needed him. A shot would bring the neighborhood down around my ears. Coppers. Publicity. Tipping my hand if the worst came to worst. But I let him have it.

The shot sounded like a cannon in that small room. He was going out the door when the bullet hit him. Where, I wasn't sure. I saw him flinch, plunge forward, and then the door slammed with force enough to take it off the hinges.

By the time I got out in the hall he was falling down the stairs three steps at a time, making enough noise to alarm the whole building. The shot had helped, too. As I charged down the hall a door opened, a man looked out at my gun with bulging eyes and ducked back.

I raced down the stairs, followed the mug outside. A man and a girl were standing on the sidewalk staring at a taxi some yards down the street.

My man was just leaping into the taxi. It sped down the street before the door was pulled shut.

At the curb my own cab was waiting.

"Follow that car!" I yelped to the driver.

But he was a cold-eyed young fellow with a mind of his own.

"Nothing doing!" he gave me. "I ain't chasing tonight. This looks sour to me an' I don't wind up in no jug for a lousy tip."

"This is police business, you idiot!"

"Lemme see your badge?"

He knew the answers. I didn't have a badge that would

count with him. And while we jawed, the other car turned the next corner and was gone.

"You ought to be pushing a banana cart!" I snarled at my driver. "Did you notice the number of that hack?"

"Nix, brother. Why should I? Hustle you a gorilla if you're putting some guy on the spot. I've got a family to go home to."

I sent him home to his family without a tip. He gave me a dirty look as he drove away.

THE YOUNG COUPLE were still staring. Two women were leaning out of front windows overhead. I was fit to tie as I walked over to the couple.

"Where did the young woman go who ran out ahead of that man? In the taxi?"

She hugged his arm, shrank from me. Maybe I was wild-eyed. I had a right to be. He answered nervously.

"No woman came out. The man was the only one—and he almost knocked us down. What's the matter?"

"It's a game," I said. "About this time every night I run friends out of their apartments. You sure a woman didn't come out?"

"Positive."

They edged toward the door; and I knew I'd get nothing but trouble hanging around. That shot had the place buzzing like a hive of bees. Ten to one a radio police car was on the way already.

I left.

Walking around the corner, I dodged up the first alley, through to the next street, and hailed a taxi a few minutes later.

"Uptown," I said, and as it rolled I sat back and called myself names.

I'd had my fist on things there at the Haddon Arms. The girl knew plenty. The big mug who had come in knew even more. Now they were both gone. I was stymied again.

I went up to the Blaine office, which never closed.

Trixie Meehan was there. Little Trixie, powdering her nose, looking demure, helpless.

"And here's the big breeze, with the answers all buttoned up in his watch pocket," Trixie yawned.

"Lay off," I snarled. "I'm having my own troubles!"

"You thrill me, Mike. What happened to curdle you?"

I told her.

Trixie listened intently.

"Too bad," she said thoughtfully. "I wonder where that girl went—and what she's going to do?"

"Wondering won't help. Where's Thompson?"

"Gone out for a sandwich."

"I hope he stays. He'll only hit the ceiling."

Trixie gave me a bleak look. And the telephone on Thompson's desk rang.

"More trouble," I growled.

"You never can tell," Trixie murmured, lifting the receiver. She listened a minute, said: "Watch it." And put the telephone down and gave me a faint smile.

"That was the man who is watching Eldridge!"

"What of it?"

Trixie put little fingers before a yawn.

"Nothing much, I suppose. He just wanted to report a woman who entered Eldridge's house. She was hatless and wore no coat and was half walking, half running. She looked, he said, as if something was on her mind."

"Did she wear a blue dress?"

"I should know. He didn't say."

I started for the door.

"Mike, where are you going?"

"To Eldridge's apartment."

"And so am I," said Trixie. And came along.

No use trying to stop her. But we jawed all the way over to Riverside Drive.

"Keep out of this," I snarled. "You'll ball it up!"

"No worse than you've done already," Trixie came back acidly.

She had me there.

"Anyway," I said, "I'm going to see Eldridge. Outside for you. I don't want him to mug you."

"Fair enough, Mike. But I'll be down the street with both ears stretched."

Our man was in a car several doors away.

"Did the woman have on a blue dress?" I asked him.

"Sort of blue. She went by here talking to herself. Sounded all upset."

"I'll bet, if Mike knows her," said Trixie. "Go stretch your legs, Cassidy. I'll sit in the car and watch. Mike's going in."

I left them there and rang Eldridge's door bell.

A BUTLER OR a servant should have answered. A big house like this rated service. It took three hard rings to get anything and then I batted my eyes when Eldridge himself opened the door.

He looked startled, then frowned, and said: "What do you want?"

His welcome would have charged an ice box.

"Something important to talk over with you, Mr. Eldridge."

I was halfway through the door when his tall, stooped figure barred my way. The same brown suit which needed pressing hung loosely on him, but I'd have taken an oath that his thin face was paler than usual. The rimless eyeglasses were gone. He peered at me near-sightedly.

But the chilly, gray eyes were colder than ever. Colder, more ruthless, as Eldridge said harshly:

"Don't come in until you're asked! I'll talk with you here at the door!"

If he'd said anything but that I might have listened to reason. Not knowing I was aware of his visitor, he was covering up. But I wasn't being kept out just then.

"Sorry," says I cheerfully. "Got to come in. This is important. Can't settle it here at the door."

And I pushed in another step before his hand shoved against my chest.

"Get out! I don't want you in here! I can't talk with you just now!"

"I'll bet you can, Eldridge."

"I don't want you in here!"

He was angry, but I've seen angry men before. He was shaken, upset, a bit frightened, too. Every word he spoke put him in a worse light. I wondered—who wouldn't?— what his hookup was with the girl of the Haddon Arms. Why should he want to conceal her presence in his house?

Crowding against his hand, I got clear in and shut the door behind me.

"Too bad, Mr. Eldridge. I'm on a case for you—and you refuse to discuss an important angle of it. It looks queer."

"Get out!" he cried furiously.

"Sure—after we talk. I want to see that young woman who came in here a few minutes ago."

His cold gray eyes blazed with madness and desperation. He grabbed me by the shoulders, threw me back against the door.

"I've had enough of this!" he panted. "Get out and stay out!"

Ducking, I eeled clear. He followed me in a stumbling rush, swearing frantically under his breath as he caught my throat.

You could have knocked me over with a pinfeather. Vice-presidents of big corporations didn't act this way. Eldridge was in a killing frenzy. It was in his eyes as my head went back and I gagged and tried to tear his hands away.

He was stronger, wiry, bigger, heavier. If he got me down, there was no telling what would happen. So I gave him a knee hard in the groin.

He groaned, bent double with the pain. His grip slackened; and I tore his hands away, stepped back and threw a right cross to his jaw with all my weight behind it.

He dropped.

The house was silent. Eldridge's loud voice should have brought help, but no servants had appeared. The uncanny quiet was foreboding. Patsy Ryan from the Haddon Arms hadn't appeared, either. That was strange, too. She had proved she was willing to mix in trouble.

So I looked around.

The house was an old one, big rooms, high ceilings. It was furnished in a period style, Louis XIV, I think. Spidery furniture with a great deal of hand carving and brocade. Tapestries hung on the walls. Dull, stiff and formal, it made a perfect setting for Eldridge.

I didn't get to see much of the house. The drawing room was off the hall to the right—and when I walked in there and turned on the light, I saw why Eldridge was so frantic to get me out of the house.

Miss Patsy Ryan was lying on a couch across the room.

She seemed to be sleeping. But we had made enough noise to wake a dead woman. No, not quite that; for when I walked to the couch and looked closer I saw that Patsy Ryan was dead.

9

A FORTUNE—TO FORGET

THE GRIEF, THE haunted look of desperation had gone from her face. One arm hung limply down to the floor. The other was crossed over her chest. I lifted it. The still warm flesh had a lifeless feeling. The arm fell limply when I released it.

Then on her neck I saw the answer. Blue-black finger-marks stood out starkly on the soft white skin. Patsy Ryan had been throttled as Eldridge had tried to throttle me.

Lying on the floor by a highly varnished table was the small automatic she had taken from her bureau drawer. Near it on the rug were the remains of Eldridge's rimless nose glasses. They had been stepped on.

A groan issued from the hall. I went there.

Eldridge was stirring on the floor. Gun in hand I waited.

His eyes opened, stared up at me. Recognition flashed in them. Then fright. He sat up with an effort, fingering his squarish jaw.

"Get up!" I told him.

Unsteadily he obeyed.

"You—you knocked me out," he muttered.

"Too bad that was all. I should have handed you what you gave that girl in there."

The terror swept back over his face. In that moment he wasn't the man of power. Fright does things to some people which are not good to look at. So to Eldridge now. Lines deepened in his thin face; it became ugly, repellent, as his eyes wandered from me to the drawing room and back again.

"You—you found her?" he stammered.

"What did you think I'd do? Walk by her?"

Fingering his jaw, he gave me a hunted look. He tried to speak. His throat was tight, his mouth wouldn't work. He got it out finally in a croak.

"She—she came here to kill me!"

"Sure—she came here to kill you—and so you killed her. Nothing else you could have done, of course."

"N-nothing," he stammered.

Funny—I believed him, and had no pity for him. Something like that had been on her face when she rushed from her room. But he could have met it differently.

"Why did you kill her?" I demanded.

"I—there was nothing else to do."

"Hand me another, Eldridge. You got the gun out of her hand. You had her helpless or you couldn't have choked her to death. Why didn't you stop when you had her helpless?"

He moistened his lips. "I—"

"You killed her," I guessed, "because you were afraid of her. Not because of what she might do with that gun she brought."

His head wagged denial. But his eyes, his face, his manner confirmed it. Without her gun Eldridge would still have been afraid of her, have wanted to kill her. Things were beginning to tie in, but I needed a lot of answers yet.

"Spit it out," I said. "How did you two hook up? What brought her here? What did she have on you?"

"N-nothing," Eldridge groaned.

He was shaky, uncertain, terrified. His eyes searched my face. A gleam of hope came into them. "How much money do you make a year?"

"Enough to live on."

"It can't be much."

MY GRIN WAS nasty.

"Eldridge," I said, "I *thought* you were going to wave money under my nose. Got a lot of it, haven't you? I ought to have some of it—if I'm willing to be reasonable."

"A man," said Eldridge, hoarsely, "can always use money."

"You should tell me. How much do you figure I need?"

Hope grew in his face.

"Ten thousand," he offered eagerly.

I grinned again. "Trying to insult me, Eldridge? What could I do with ten thousand dollars?"

"Fifteen—no, twenty! Twenty thousand *cash!*"

And the hope grew on his face. I guess he couldn't figure a man turning down cash money. Not that much. Some of his poise, assurance, returned.

"Twenty thousand, Eldridge, to keep you from burning in the chair? *Tut, tut;* is that all you're worth?"

He gulped.

"Thirty thousand, Harris. I haven't it here, of course, but I'll give it to you as soon as the banks open in the morning."

"Would you go fifty thousand?"

He didn't bat an eye.

"If you'll do business for that, I'll pay it!"

"I'll bet you would," I sighed. "Fifty grand. That's a lot of dough. I could retire on that with what I've got saved."

"That's right. You can take it easy, Harris. Travel. Be your own boss."

I laughed at him.

"Sure I could—but I won't. You're not the first dirty crook who's waved cash under my nose, Eldridge. I could have retired long ago if I'd taken half the bribes. If they can prove you killed that girl—and I think they can— you're going to the chair, as sure as God made little fishes. And now what have you been covering up about Bronson—while you've been running around with Bronson's wife?"

He winced. How he hated me in that moment. It blazed from his face.

"How—how much do you know?" he asked in a shaking voice.

"Plenty. You'll get a load of it at the trial."

"And—you won't take cash to forget this? A fortune?"

"No."

Just then the front door shoved hurriedly open behind me. Big, heavy, that door edge struck me in the back and knocked me off balance. And Eldridge, with utter desperation making a drawn mask of his face, moved quicker than I thought possible.

He was on me like a cat, heedless of what might happen.

Off balance, I couldn't dodge. My gun had shifted. His left hand knocked it further out. And his right caught me on the side of the face and snapped my head back against the sharp edge of the door.

I knew that afterwards.

At the moment all I knew was Eldridge's fist almost in my face—and behind me the low, startled cry of a woman. Not Trixie. The next instant everything did a blackout.

10

A DEAD MAN WALKS

I OPENED MY eyes and could not see.

My hands were pawing weakly toward my face. A cold, chill feeling was raising gooseflesh. Something furry and alive had scuttled hastily off my face as my eyes opened.

I sat up with pulses pounding, breathing short.

I remembered—Eldridge—his fist—the woman's cry of fear—and a gap until now. I was conscious, wide awake, but I couldn't see anything.

Exploring fingers found a long, blood-matted gash in the back of my head. I recalled the sharp edge of the door just behind me. That explained the blackout. Hard to tell how long I had been unconscious.

I was not tied. I had been lying on my back, on cold metal covered with small particles of dirt.

The quiet was the quiet of death. The air was chill, tanged with a sourish smell. I shivered, stood up, swaying dizzily. The blackness was so thick I could almost feel it pressing in.

"I took a step ahead, then another more confidently; but on the third my toe struck an obstruction which almost tripped me.

Exploring, I found a metal strip extending up from the metal floor. Beyond it there was no floor. As far down as

I could reach was only space—into which I had almost fallen.

Taking a coin from my pocket, I pitched it into the void. It struck far below. Faint scurryings came up through the blackness, shrill squeaks.

That explained the movement on my face as I came out of the stupor. Rats. I had a real chill then. I've always hated rats.

Matches, cigarettes, bill fold, wrist watch—everything had been taken from my pockets but the small change. Foot by foot I explored along the metal stripping which bounded the void. My shoes crunched on brittle particles. Rats continued to scurry in the darkness, squealing now and then.

My foot struck something soft, and I guessed what it was before I stooped and touched rough cloth—and then a face. No comfort there. The flesh was set, hard, clammy, cold. I snatched my hand away, swearing under my breath.

The short hairs at the back of my neck were prickling as I skirted the body. Death was in the air. Then a wall, a metal wall, damp, cold. From it a metal rib projected; a short distance to the right was another metal rib; then another, equally spaced.

And I chuckled out loud with sudden relief. I knew where I was. Those ribs were part of a ship's hull. I had almost fallen over a hatch coaming, down into the ship's hold. No wonder everything was black, silent. Broken only by the squeals of rats. The sour smell came from some past cargo.

At least I hadn't been shanghaied. The ship's engines

were not working. I was somewhere along the waterfront; probably over on the Jersey side.

This made sense, tying back to the Hugger gang. Eldridge had a line into them. The Sin Doctor had been righter than he suspected.

Metal clanged and I jumped. Some distance away a small patch of light opened in the blackness. Peering, blinking, I saw forms in the light. One seemed to be a woman, who was roughly shoved through the door.

A gruff voice reverberated hollowly.

"If you won't talk, stay in there with the rats until we're ready for you!"

The metal door clanged shut. Through the darkness the woman's voice came furiously.

"A whip is what they need!"

"Trixie!" I called.

"Mike!"

"Watch your step," I warned. "I almost fell through an open hatch a few minutes ago."

"Mike—I thought you were dead! They said you were dead!"

"Do I sound like it?"

"N-no, Mike. But I won't believe it until I get my hands on you."

"Get your hands ready, darling. I'm coming."

We met in the blackness and I caught Trixie's hands. They were cold, shaky.

"What happened?" I asked her. "Eldridge knocked my head against the front door—and I just came out of it."

"You were right, Mike. I should have stayed at the office.

I might have been some good to you there. That—that
Bronson woman tricked me."

It took a lot to make Trixie so meek. I didn't feel like
wisecracking myself. Neither of us did.

"SO THAT WAS Bronson's wife who opened the front
door?" I said.

"Yes. She walked past the car. I didn't think she recognized me; and so when she came back and said you wanted
to see me, I swallowed it and went with her. Eldridge
grabbed me as soon as I got inside. You were lying there
on the floor with the back of your head all bloody. Eldridge
tied me and gagged me. In a few minutes an automobile
brought several men. They took us out to the car. We rode
somewhere to the water front, got in a boat and went quite
a distance. I don't know where this ship is lying, Mike.
They've had me up in one of the cabins, trying to make
me talk. They want to know how much we know. They told
me you were dead—and that I'd go in the bay after you if
I didn't talk."

I patted Trixie's shoulder. "We're still kicking, kid. We'll
wangle it someway. Got any matches?"

"No."

"Have to go it blind then. Don't be surprised if you step
on a dead man. I did."

"A d-dead man in here with us?" Trixie faltered.

"Dead as he'll ever be. He can't hurt you—and he may
help us."

Trixie sniffed, said: "If we have to wait for a dead man
to get us out, we might as well give up now."

I chuckled.

"Dead man or not, he's going to work for us. Wait here."

I felt my way back to the body, lifted it by the shoulders. Gruesome? You bet. If you've never wrestled a corpse in a deserted ship's hold with rats scampering about, you have no idea. I had gooseflesh, chills, shaking knees and cold sweat. But we waltzed, that corpse and I, back to the bulkhead door.

I propped him up there beside the door. He was going to perform one good deed in death, no matter what he had done in life. Rigid in *rigor mortis,* he stayed upright.

And I turned back and searched through the blackness.

My foot finally struck a sizable chunk of coal. I put it down beside the stranger's feet, feeling almost chummy toward him. Queer how danger blunts one's emotion.

"Here, sweetness," I says to Trixie.

"Not me!" Trixie answered firmly. "You've got that dead man there!"

"Uh-huh. He's friendly. Snap out of it. Want to get out of here or not?"

"Do I?" says Trixie. She edged through the darkness and grabbed my arm. In a whisper I told her what was on my mind.

Trixie listened carefully. No hysteria about her even now. In a pinch you could always count on her.

When I finished, she warned: "It's dangerous, Mike."

"Dangerous to stay here, too. If you're not having any of it, slip to the other end and lie low!"

"Listen, Ape!" says Trixie indignantly. "If you're insane enough to try it, I'm insane enough to go along. It can't be much worse than this. They're pretty bad, Mike. I think it's the harbor for us in the end. We know too much. Eldridge has a say here—and he can't afford to have us show up and talk."

I patted Trixie's shoulder. "Good girl. We'll have to wait."

So we waited. How those minutes dragged. It was cruel. We talked some in whispers, but for the most part we were silent.

Steps finally sounded beyond the steel door. A lock was removed. I straightened with the chunk of coal in my hand.

"All set?" I whispered.

"You bet!" Trixie answered.

The door swung out. A flashlight glared through.

"Get in there!" a gruff voice ordered.

A hard shove sent a man staggering in. Over the low sill behind him followed the man with the light. I glimpsed a gun in his other hand. And the corpse jumped at him.

IT SOUNDS BAD. It was worse. That hoodlum with the flashlight met horror, cold stiff horror. I shivered myself as his light silvered a cold white face, staring eyes, stiff arms half raised. Trixie, half hidden behind the body, had done her part well. The corpse seemed to lunge in attack.

He squawked like a startled rooster. His gun lifted—and I brought down the heavy lump of coal on his head. It shattered—and he went down under the dead man.

Behind me a choked voice said: "Damnation! That you, Mike?"

"Yep. Cassidy?"

"It's me," Cassidy said. "When I got back to the car two men put guns on me an' hustled me away. Car an' all. I don't know what it was all about. The rats put me through plenty before they sent me down here."

Cassidy was tall and angular. The flashlight showed him

disheveled, pale, hot-eyed now. His face was bruised and cut by blows. He still looked rather dizzy.

"Where are we?" I asked him.

"In the bay," Cassidy said. "This tub is anchored. There's no dock around that I could see. Plenty water and foghorns in the distance."

It took me a moment to figure that out. No docks. An anchored hulk, for if there was steam up on this boat I was a liar.

"Smart," I said under my breath. "I'll bet we're around the anchorage below Governor's Island, off the Bush Terminal. Who'd ever think of looking on one of those boats? Not even the harbor cops, I'll bet, as long as everything looks quiet on their decks."

"Ummmm—maybe," Cassidy said doubtfully.

Beyond the door a hollow voice called down from above: "Going to take all night down there, Steve?"

"Okay," I answered gruffly; and under my breath said to Cassidy: "Come along. Hang back now and you'll join that dead man."

"Sure," Cassidy agreed.

Steel grating lay beyond the bulkhead door. I slammed the door noisily, snapped the lock, climbed up a ladder of the grating, keeping the light away from Cassidy and Trixie, who followed behind.

We seemed to be over the fireroom. Overhead, as we went up, the same voice complained: "You must 'a' been throwin' a party with that dame down there."

I climbed with the gun Cassidy's guard had carried. Two flights of ladders—and more steel grating at the top.

Cassidy and Trixie were just behind me, still hidden in the darkness.

My flash shone on a short, stocky man waiting just inside the deck door. I'd seen him before, at Pier 49 that afternoon. He was one of the three who had chased me ashore.

He scowled in the light, snarled. "Douse that! Hugger'll take you apart for lettin' light out on deck!"

He still couldn't see Cassidy and Trixie—but he heard their steps—As I snapped the light out and moved to him, he blurted: "Who's that behind you?"

11

THE ATTACK

MY AUTOMATIC JAMMED deep in his stomach. I crowded him back against the wall. My forearm hit his throat, knocking his head back to the wall.

"*Quiet!*" says I. "One yip and you get it!"

He caught the idea. I think he forgot to breathe for a moment.

Cassidy was at my side a moment later, frisking him.

"Here's an automatic," Cassidy whispered.

"Give it to Trixie. She's got to have something if this blows up."

"Thanks, Mike," said Trixie in a small voice.

I grabbed a handful of the mug's throat. "Where are we?"

"Below Governor's Island," he gagged.

"How many men aboard here?"

"Eleven."

"Where's Bronson?"

Silence.

So I choked him until he retched.

"Sweetheart," says I, "I'll beat your face in with this gun in thirty seconds. Where's Bronson?"

He understood that kind of English, all right.

"Locked in one of the cabins," he stammered.

Cassidy whispered with cold ferocity.

"Lemme at him! He's one of the guys who worked on me! I'll kill him, s'help me!"

Ever have a whisper chill you? Cassidy's did me. He meant it. Crazy, cold mad, he would have throttled the fellow right there. That mug trembled in my grip.

"Nix!" I told Cassidy. "If he talks, give him a chance."

And I choked the fellow again.

"Who shot that man in the chauffeur's uniform who was lamming in a boat? The one named Tony?" I asked. "And how come the trouble was up river—and now we're down here in the bay?"

I was half sure of the answer. He gave it to me.

"Tony got Hugger into it," he blurted through stiff lips. "Tony's girl was thick with a guy who was willing to lay dough to have Bronson snatched an' kept out of the way. He cut us in—an' then Hugger figures there's more money in it by makin' Bronson pay to get out. Hugger plays for a wad; an' Tony gets mad an' says he's through; an' Hugger locks him up; an Tony knifes the guy who's watchin' him an' starts across the river from the Jersey side. We was up there then. Hugger goes after him shootin', an' lost him; so he goes to Tony's girl, figuring Tony'll duck in there.

"An' Tony's dead an' the girl's crazy. She figures Tony's been double-crossed someway. She goes for the guy who put up the dough for Bronson's snatching, an' he gets her gun away an' she says she's going to blow the lid off to Centre Street. The cops would tear everything wide open. That guy goes screwy himself at the idea an' kills her right there. An' now Hugger's tryin' to figure an out for it all."

"I'll bet," says I. "Here's an out for you." I slugged him

with the gun and he went down without a sound. "One down in the hold and one here," I said to Cassidy. "That leaves nine. And if we can find Bronson and get him ashore, we can call it a day."

"To hell with Bronson! You're nuts! Let's get off this boat. We can come back with help."

"And no dice on Bronson then. Do you think they'll keep him around here if we get away? They moved him once tonight when trouble broke out. I've got an idea."

"It'll have to be a good one," Cassidy said sourly.

"It is. Trixie, you willing to take a chance?"

Without hesitation Trixie says, "I've taken worse. Lead on, Ape." So I led them out on deck. The wet fog still swirled past, thicker down here in the bay. Our shoes padded softly. No lights were visible, no sounds audible. Water slapped the boat's side with soft, ghostlike sounds. We might have been on a deserted derelict.

I flicked the light once or twice to see the way. The ship was a small cargo boat. A hatch was placed back of the bridge superstructure, cutting bridge and captain's quarters off from the amidship's part. Under the bridge, where the captain's quarters would be, a thread of light glowed around a closed porthole.

WE EDGED UP a companion ladder, listened outside the door. Men were talking upside. A harsh voice I recognized was saying:

"By God, they got to go over the side! This guy Eldridge is wild. We'll all burn if they get back."

"How about Bronson, Hugger?"

The gorilla with the face like a chunk of raw meat—the one who had crashed the Greenwich Village apartment—

was the man known as Tom Hugger, who ran the gang. And he growled:

"Damn Bronson! He don't know nothing! He was still dopy when we moved him down here this evening. He can go back an' shoot his mouth off all he likes an' it can't touch us. He ain't seen any of us but Tony. That rat's dead an' so's his girl. Even the watchman on this tub is down in the bunker dead. We're in the clear, I tell you—an' this guy Eldridge is good for a shakedown every now an' then for years. If he comes out of this settin' pretty, he'll pay big dough to keep it quiet."

Another voice growled: "Let's get those three up here an' make 'em talk. The two guys will come through if we start workin' on the girl. And then we can tie grate bars to them and the watchman and toss them over the side. Bronson will kick through to be put ashore. He's going soft now."

Maybe my next move wasn't sane. I felt a bit insane after hearing what was in store for Trixie. These harbor hoodlums had gone wild with murder—and I was wild myself as I opened the door and jumped inside with the automatic ready.

Four of them were seated in there in the light of two lanterns. You could have cut the tobacco smoke with a knife.

A couple of bottles were open. They had been drinking. They all looked as I came in—and for a moment were too surprised to move.

"Put 'em up! It's a pinch!"

Gimpy Lewis was among them, young, scrawny, with a doped-up glitter in his eyes. He went for his gun. I shot him.

They could understand that. Gimpy Lewis went to the floor coughing, hugging his stomach. And they didn't know how many men were outside. Three pairs of hands went up in the air. Tom Hugger's too. He was as ugly as ever, as dangerous—but his meaty hands went up too.

"How'd you get up here?" he snarled.

"I flew up, sweetheart," says I. "Cassidy, get their rods! Trixie, come in here and shut the door."

Cassidy looked ugly too as he stepped past me and frisked them. I breathed easier as soon as he had a gun in his hand. Surprised, they had been easy for a moment; but that shot would bring trouble. We'd have trouble.

Hugger was already figuring on it. His face was lumpy with hate and readiness. God help us if we slipped up now.

Hugger spoke through his teeth. "They ain't no coppers out there! These three busted out someway!"

"And what a bust, sweetheart," I grinned. "Keep quiet—or you'll draw the next one."

His mouth tightened but the muscles stood out in his cheeks. He was thinking hard, still dangerous. That kind of guy doesn't fold up.

Trixie slammed the door. "They're coming, Mike! I hear them running!"

So there we were, bottled up with five hoodlums outside. I knew then I had been crazy to try this—but it was too late to do anything about it now.

12

FOOL'S PARADISE

HUGGER GRINNED. HE was thinking the same thing, I was. He knew we were trapped. He was waiting now.

We all jumped as a brace of shots blasted outside and one of the glass portholes splintered in. They had opened the iron cover, shot the glass out. Now they could pick Cassidy and I off at their leisure.

"Get behind these guys!" I yelled to Cassidy—and jumped for the nearest man as a third shot crashed through the porthole.

The bullet grazed my side. That quick jump had saved my life. Trixie was braced flat against the opposite wall under one of the portholes.

On the deck outside a voice yelled: "Come out with your hands in the air or we'll let you have it!"

"Now we can laugh," I called from behind my man.

But I was bluffing. We couldn't hold this long. Somebody would figure an out—if only to get Bronson off the ship. I thought fast. We were in the captain's cabin. There was a door in the back wall. I guessed it would open into the chart room.

From the chart room there would be steps up to the

wheel house and the bridge. We could get up there—and then what?

I spoke to Hugger. "Run 'em away or I'll put a bullet in you!"

He sneered at me.

"Fat chance! They're running things out on deck now."

He was not telling me, but was giving orders to the men outside.

"Slide over here behind me," I said to Trixie.

As she obeyed, a face popped up at a porthole. I shot at it, hit the steel porthole rim. The face disappeared.

"Cassidy, you and Trixie get through this door behind me. I'll cover you."

Cassidy obeyed, passing me an extra gun as he went, and calling back: "It's the chart room."

So I put my gun on Hugger and took him into the chart room with me.

He went like a surly bear, watching his chance for a break—and didn't get it. Stairs led up to the wheel house. No one had thought to come down this way and get at us from behind. Cassidy went up first, then Trixie, and I followed with my gun in Hugger's back.

And we heard a yell on deck.

"Watch for 'em, boys! They'll put the finger on us if they get away!"

We were in the wheel house when the same voice yelled: "They're up on the bridge! Rush 'em!"

"Put your gun in this man's back!" I snapped to Trixie. "Cassidy, take the port side! I'll take the other side."

And I ran to the head of the starboard companion ladder

in time to meet a rush of steps up through the fog-filled blackness.

I shot down blindly, jumped to one side, crouched. A man yelled. I heard him tumble back to the deck. Men cursed down there in the darkness. A burst of shots raked the spot where I had been standing.

Cassidy fired twice beyond the wheel house. The firing continued from the deck. Little spurts of flame marked the guns. Bullets smashed into the wheel house, zipped through the sides of the bridge.

I was down flat on my stomach by then, hoping that Cassidy was doing the same, thankful that Trixie was sheltered behind the wheel house. I hoped she'd kill Hugger if he made a move.

The shooting slackened off. I heard the click of fresh clips being inserted in automatics.

"All right, Cassidy?" I called.

"Yeah!"

From the deck below a man called: "Toss your rods down here an' we'll let you go!"

"Come up and get 'em!" I invited.

We couldn't see them. They couldn't see us. Kicking off my shoes, I slipped over to the wheel house and climbed up on top. Just as I got there the same speaker yelled:

"Rush 'em again, boys! They can't shoot long!"

He fired as he spoke. I saw the flash—and emptied the last shots in one of my automatics at the spot. He screamed, floundered around down there by the hatch—and they did no rushing for a moment.

BUT HE HAD been right about our guns. Trixie would need hers. We couldn't stand them off long; when our shells ran out we would be cold meat for them. Thought of the lapping harbor made me shiver—and the shiver was more for Trixie than myself. That game little girl deserved better than that.

"Mike!" Trixie called. "You all right?"

"Sitting pretty," I answered from the top of the wheel house.

The next instant I wasn't sitting pretty. Down there on deck guns cut loose at me. Splinters flew from the edge of the wheel house, bullets missed me by a hair. I flopped down flat, felt lead ripping through the roof all around me. The wheel house walls couldn't stop all those big automatic bullets.

Funny, in that moment I worried most about Trixie not being safe after all.

A bullet creased my leg. A splinter gashed my cheek. It was butchery, and I didn't even have enough bullets to shoot back. Cassidy fired twice—and we had that many less shots to hold them off.

Then I heard Trixie's gun go off. She cried something—I couldn't catch it—and then Hugger's voice bawled something at the top of the starboard companion ladder. He was a free man—and God knew what harm he had brought to Trixie. I went mad at that moment.

His shoes slammed on the ladder as I whirled to the edge of the wheel house roof to put my last shots down at him. The men on deck heard it too. I guess they thought it was Cassidy or me. Two of them opened up at the ladder.

He bellowed: *"Hold it! It's me, Hug—"*

They never heard who it was—but I guess they knew

by the time Hugger hit the deck. A stricken silence fell. A shaking voice groaned:

"Gawd—you hit Hugger!"

"Laugh that off!" I yelled.

That drew one half-hearted shot. In the silence which followed, speeding engines burst through the fog near the ship. The ghostly beam of a powerful searchlight waved toward us. It found the ship, stopped over the deck, getting brighter as it sheered in close.

"The cops!"

I knew it before that yell of alarm came from below. Those shots on the open deck had carried out over the water.

A cruising patrol boat had heard them. My idea of getting out in the open had worked out after all.

There were no more shots. They dashed under the bridge, down on the forward deck, and I heard them scrambling over the rail down to a waiting boat.

The searchlight swept around the bow, stabbed down that side just in time to pick out the last two men going over the rail.

Bawled commands drifted through the fog. Engines backed hard, raced again. The patrol boat turned on a dime and surged in toward the ship's side as I came down off the wheel house.

Trixie wailed: "Mike, I didn't mean to let him get away! A bullet went past my ear and I dodged. He slapped his hand back and knocked the gun away and knocked me down and ran."

"You did well enough, Baby," says I, patting Trixie's little shoulder. "You held him while it counted. He won't run away any more. Come over here and watch the show from a box seat. We're going to get a rest."

"And that," said Cassidy behind us with vast relief, "is the best thing I've heard tonight. They had me doubtful for awhile."

SO WE WENT to the wing of the bridge and looked down through the fog as the police boat crowded the launch in against the side of the ship and took that load of hoodlums over the side under the muzzles of machine guns.

An officer led men aboard. We went down to meet them. In the glare of flashlights one of the men recognized me.

"It's the little guy who brought that body in tonight!" he exclaimed.

I grinned, the first time I had really felt like it that evening.

"I've got a few more for you," I told them. "And there's a man locked up aboard here who wants to be out bad."

We found Bronson in one of the officers' cabins. A fire ax broke the door in. Bronson lurched out, a chunky, grizzled man, unshaven, pale and wobbly by what he had been through. If he had been doped, the effects had worn off, been shocked away by the gunfire.

"Thank God!" he exclaimed. "I didn't think there was a chance of anyone finding me. What date is this?"

I told him; and told him who I was.

He looked relieved. "You came in time."

"In time for what? You might as well have it now, Mr. Bronson. Eldridge was behind this."

"Eldridge? So!" said Bronson—and it was plain that Eldridge was through forever with the Bronson Steamship and Navigation Company.

"I have a big deal on—a merger," Bronson explained hurriedly. "I've options enough on the other company's stock to vote control. But if I'm not there personally for the meeting tomorrow I lose out and a small fortune besides. If Eldridge was behind this, he was trying to throw a monkey wrench in my plans. I'll settle him in the morning. Gentlemen, can you get me to where I can get word to my wife? She—she's probably prostrated by this."

The coppers didn't know. I didn't tell Bronson about his wife. But as Trixie and I waited while the coppers took the wounded and dead off, I spoke regretfully, thinking of Bronson's wife.

"Some men live in a fool's paradise."

"And why not?" says little Trixie. "Most *men* are fools."

That started it. We were still scrapping when the police boat docked.

THE CITY HALL MURDERS

*A Little Box of Deadly Secrets, Two
Words Gasped by a Dying Man, Put
Mike Harris on the Trail of Death
That Stalked Through City Hall*

1

KILLER'S RECKONING

I SAW BENNY PARKER die. The sight wasn't pretty. It tied me up inside, hit me harder than anything which had happened since I had been with the Blaine International Agency. Plenty had happened in those years too.

I'm Mike Harris, not so big, not so hot, even if my hair is red. But I get around and the Blaine Agency covers about every kind of dirt. Still Benny Parker's death hit me hard.

Benny wasn't the kind who was cut out to die. He was only a kid, a blond, grinning kid who had a trick of whistling funny little tunes that pulled the corners of your mouth up to match Benny's grin and made you feel that maybe things weren't so bad after all.

It wasn't the whistle. It was Benny. You liked the kid on sight and kept on liking him.

Maybe that was why Thompson put Benny on the payroll of the Blaine Agency. It couldn't have been because Benny was a dick. He wasn't—then. I was in New York at the time and saw some of Benny's breaking-in. At first he didn't know what it was all about.

Thompson, the boss of the eastern division, probably figured that angle. Benny didn't look like a dick, didn't act like one, and I guess nobody took the trouble to hide anything from him. From the first he had a way of getting information.

In two years Benny made good with a bang and grew better. So when Thompson assigned me to help Benny neither of us figured it was more than a yawn.

Thompson told me that morning in New York: "Better hop over to Middleton, Pennsylvania, and see what's the matter with Benny Parker. I just received a wire from him asking for another man."

"What's Benny doing in Middleton?" I asked Thompson.

"Don't know," says Thompson, chewing on his unlighted cigar. "Last week the mayor of the town long-distanced in for a good man. Benny was the only one I had free that day, so I sent him."

"How big is Middleton?"

"Search me," says Thompson.

So I took his atlas off the bookshelf and looked. Forty-eight thousand. Not such a bad little town at that. I was interested as I put the book back.

"Will you tell me why the mayor of a burg listed at forty-eight thousand in the last census is yelping for a private dick from New York?" I asked Thompson. "He's got a neat little police force of his own. Probably a couple of private detectives around. If he's curious about anything, why doesn't he use local talent?"

"If I knew," says Thompson, "I'd tell you."

"And if I knew," I gave Thompson back, "I'd feel a damned sight less curious than I am right now. It sounds screwy to me."

"Since when are you worrying about who pays the agency bill?" Thompson grunted.

That was Thompson all over. He was a dick and nothing else. The Blaine Agency was sunrise and sunset to Thompson. He would have investigated a case for the devil if he had been certain of money for the bill. Probably would have anyway, and let the cashier's department do the worrying about that end of it.

So I asked Thompson only one more thing. "What's Benny's address?"

"God knows," Thompson yawned. "But this is his telephone number." He looked at a memorandum slip, copied a number off, handed it to me. "Call this from the station and Benny will tell you what to do."

So I went to Middleton with Benny Parker's telephone number and an overnight bag.

BENNY WAS IN when I telephoned from the old red brick station. His sigh of relief rolled out of the telephone receiver.

"I'm mighty glad Thompson sent you, Mike. I think you're just the man for the job. God knows I need you."

"What's wrong?"

Benny answered nervously.

"Can't tell you over the telephone, Mike. I was just starting to the mayor's office. Meet me there and I'll give you the lowdown."

So I checked my bag, hopped in a hack and told the driver to take me to the mayor's office. The car was a broken-down city cab which had been banished to the sticks for the last few thousand miles that were in the motor before junking. The driver was a thin, hunched-shoulder gilly who threw words over his shoulder from the corner of his mouth with a wise air.

"Stranger in town?" he asks me.

"Do I look it?"

The side of his face screwed in a grin. "Any man who don't know where the mayor's office is, ain't been around town lately."

"How come?" I knew I had put myself wide open as soon as I said it.

The gilly grinned again. His mouth had a trick of turning up until it seemed to cut halfway to his cheekbone.

"If you'd been around at all, you'd 'a' read enough in the paper to know all about the mayor's office an' the new city hall," he said.

I let it go at that, not so steamed up over the fact that I'd let a hacker spot me as a stranger ten minutes after I hit town. It might be all right, and again it might not. You

never could tell in this business. Little things had a way of growing into big things so fast it made you dizzy.

Middleton was a queer combination, half old, half new. You've seen that kind of town. New suburbs, modern houses on the outskirts, shading in to older, shabbier neighborhoods near the center.

But the business district had been pepped up. New store

He picked up a chair to crash through the window.

and office buildings, new street paving and a general air of up-an'-at-'em prosperity.

Main Street—yes, it was called that—gave me part of the answer.

Politics.

What the boys had done was a crime to the eye and probably a worse crime to the town's pocketbook.

A whole city block had evidently been razed and someone had shaken down a fat contract to reincarnate a bit of old Greece. White limestone had been piled lavishly. Pillars, frescoes, wide vistas of steps and marble fountains spraying water amid green lawns greeted the tourists who ambled along Main Street. And there was a ten-story tower with barred windows on the upper floors which evidently housed the jail.

All very fine and modern. Some big cities hadn't done as well—but it looked like an awful jolt to hand the taxpayers.

"THERE Y'ARE," SAYS the driver as he let me out and ripped the check from the meter. "That's the city hall an' you'll find the mayor inside on the second floor—*an'* the check is sixty cents."

I howled: "Sixty cents? Since when did you take up larceny? We haven't gone more than a mile from the station."

I'd passed up the meter. But a gander at it now showed sixty cents, which still didn't mean anything. I swung around for a big argument—and a copper rolls up in answer to the driver's signal.

"This gentleman thinks I'm slipping him a fast one on the sixty cent charge from the station, officer," says the driver. "He's a stranger in town an' ain't sure about the rates yet."

The copper was fine-looking, snappy and alert in a new uniform. He grinned at me instead of looking for an argument himself.

"Sixty cents is the regular charge from the station, mister," he tells me. "Taxi rates are a little high here in Middleton."

"High is too sweet a word for it."

But I paid without further argument. Here were two men now who knew I was a stranger in town, and one of them a lead-in to the local coppers. It was beginning to look like I might as well have hit town with a brass band and flags flying.

So the copper strolled away and the taxi rolled away and I climbed across acres of stone steps and walked into that gorgeous city hall. And right off I spotted the usual gang of city hall loafers. White limestone, marble, bronze and bubbling fountains couldn't change them.

Some had jobs, some wanted jobs, some were busted and others were in the money—but all had their eyes on the taxpayers and the taxpayers' money.

My wrist watch said three forty-five. The main corridor was bustling with movement. A crowded elevator snapped me to the second floor. Several got out there with me.

At the end of the hall I found the mayor's office. Inside the door was a sizable reception room. Six men and two women were seated there ahead of me. They looked at me stolidly, without interest. Benny wasn't among them.

A trig brunette secretary came to the railing, handed me a professional smile, asked me what I wanted.

I gave her the famous Mike Harris smile. "Believe it or not, sister, nothing."

She lifted her nose, watched me sit down, and it wasn't until she turned back to her desk that she peeled a smile to herself.

Maybe the mayor knew I was in town. Maybe not. Benny Parker might not want it out that he knew me. I'd get the slant on that when Benny walked through the door I was watching.

In ten minutes the mayor passed three callers in and out. Smooth work, for they came out smiling. But where was Benny?

Then I saw him swing into the door-way and lurch against the side of the door frame. Stunned surprise came over his face. No wonder. The two crashing shots at Benny's back almost deafened me.

2

"—WATCH BRUNETTE—!"

THOSE TWO SHOTS paralyzed everyone else in the room. I jumped for the doorway, swearing at having left my rod in my bag. It would have to happen this way.

Benny staggered out of the doorway into my arms. I had to grab him as he started to flop to the floor. Maybe you've never seen a blond, grinning kid you like a lot starting on the long one-way trip. Don't if you can get out of it.

Benny Parker wasn't grinning then. His hat had fallen off. His face had changed to a pale mask out of which his blue eyes stared with a kind of horror. With fright, as if Benny was seeing things invisible to my eyes.

But Benny knew me.

"Mike, they got me!" Benny muttered thickly as his head lopped on my shoulder.

"Take it easy, kid," I said huskily, as I lowered him quickly to the rug. "Tell me about it after I get the so-an'-so who did this!"

"Mike, wait!" Benny's voice wasn't much more than a whisper. I was kneeling on the rug beside him then. Sudden confusion in the waiting room boiled around us. Two of the women had screamed. One of them was sobbing wildly now in near hysteria.

Outside in the hall I could hear excitement. Maybe the gunman was getting away. But Benny's whisper held me kneeling there at his side.

It was that kind of a whisper. Somehow I sensed that if I didn't stay and listen to Benny I might be sorry for it.

"I'm going to die!" Benny got out with an effort.

"Hell no, kid, forget it! A doc'll be here in a minute!"

I could hear the secretary frantically telephoning police headquarters upstairs. "...*a doctor and an ambulance quickly!*" she cried.

I don't think Benny heard her—but he heard me. With an effort he got a corner of his mouth up in the old grin. Only one corner. It was pitiful.

And Benny's next words came through lips already smudging with blood.

"A doc won't do me any good, Mike. 'S getting dark. Can't—hardly—see—you. Guess—I'm going. Watch brunette...."

Benny's voice trailed off. My ear was down close to his mouth by then but I couldn't hear any more.

"Benny!" I said in his ear. "Can you hear me? I've got to know more!"

Benny's eyes were still open; but in them was only that vacuity I had seen a score of times before. Benny Parker's heart was still beating, but Benny himself had gone somewhere else.

TWO MEN KNELT down beside us. One of them was slobbering excitedly from fat lips. "Is he shot? Anything wrong with him?"

"Watch him and keep your hands off him!" I snarled, and jumped out through the doorway.

Every office along the hall had poured people out to add to the confusion. An instant later an elevator door popped open and a wave of coppers and dicks rushed toward the mayor's office.

"Get back where you came from!" the first copper yelled threateningly at me.

A second elevator door banged open and more of them broke out into the confusion.

So I let the first ones carry me back into the anteroom. Bucking the entire headquarters force of Middleton wasn't going to get me anywhere.

A square-shouldered plainclothes-man crowded in against me. A doctor with an emergency bag popped in and went to work on Benny.

But one look showed me the doctor was probably wasting his time. Benny was in a coma. Too little blood had appeared to give much hope. Benny had been shot twice in the back at close range. The damage was inside. They seldom came out of a shock like that.

My only hope now was that Benny would rally enough to tell someone—preferably me—what had been on his mind.

The fat man who had knelt excitedly beside me was plucking at the doctor's shoulders.

"How is he, doctor? Will he come out of it all right?"

Gray-haired, smooth-shaven, wise and competent, that doctor wasted little time on the questions. He shook his head as he looked up once.

"I can't be sure right now, Your Honor," he said curtly. "Will you please get back and keep quiet while I'm doing this?"

So this was His Honor! This fat, excitable fellow whose hands were shaking and eyes popping. I stood back against the wall and watched.

The doctor looked up after a moment. "I doubt if he'll pull through."

The mayor almost wrung his pudgy hands. His reply was a tragic bleat: "Oh, my God! Right here in my office!"

"What's that?" the doctor asked.

"Nothing," says the mayor hastily! "Nothing."

THE CHIEF OF police had come in person, gold-braided cap and all. He was big too. Big in a beefy way. All muscle and bone. I wondered how much of the bone was in his head as I edged near and heard him address the mayor from one side.

"What do you know about this, Your Honor?"

The mayor jumped, turned. "Oh, hello, Morgan. What do I know about this? Nothing, of course. How should I know anything? I was back in my office with a caller when it happened. Terrible, isn't it? Have you got the man who did it?"

His Honor's hands had stopped shaking. But he was still nervous. His eyes were rolling uneasily about the office. He hung on the chief's reply.

"Haven't got the fellow yet, Your Honor. But we will any minute. It'll only take a little time to search the building. As soon as we got word upstairs, all exits were blocked. We've got him in here somewhere."

The mayor moistened dry lips.

"I hope so," he said.

The chief asked: "Do you know the man? Can you tell us anything about him?"

I almost missed the mayor's instant of hesitation myself.

"He has been here several times to see me about a job," the mayor replied. "I'm afraid that's all I can tell you about him, Chief. I was doing what I could. He seemed a nice young chap."

"He did that," the chief agreed.

The ambulance doctor came in ahead of his stretcher bearers. They rushed Benny Parker away. The two medical men spoke briefly together—and that was over.

I saw one of the women point at me. The dick who had been questioning her planted himself before me.

"You saw that man shot?" he asked.

I said "Yeah," and wished he'd go away. Benny's blond, kid face was still in my mind. I didn't want to talk about it.

The copper did. "He was coming in here, wasn't he?"

"Ask me something I know," I cracked back. "I only saw him stop in the doorway. I don't know what he was going to do."

The dick topped me by a head. His face was square, shaved close, shiny. He looked honest, ponderous. I'd have bet a goldfish to a gold brick he could wield a length of garden hose in a precinct back room with skill enough to crack most tough eggs. Little tufts of hair protruded from ears and nostrils. Muscles bunched gently in his cheeks as he scowled down at me.

"Fresh guy, huh?"

"Nope," I says. "Only I don't know anything."

"What's your name?"

"Harris."

"That all?"

"Michael Harris."

I lifted my voice on the last so that the mayor could hear. He didn't give me a tumble. I knew then Benny Parker hadn't tipped the mayor off.

THE NAME DIDN'T mean anything to the dick either. He cleared his throat.

"I understand you were the first one to reach the man after he was shot."

"Somebody had to reach him."

He frowned again. A nasty tone came into his voice. "Lay off the wise cracks and answer my questions. You laid him down on the rug an' he said something to you, didn't he?"

"Did he?"

"He did!" said the copper ominously. "What'd he say?"

I could have said things to the sharp-faced woman who had pointed me out. She must have seen Benny's lips move. Probably had added to it. The coppers would leech to me now and what good would I be?"

I reached for a handkerchief, wiped my eyes.

"Officer," I choked, "that poor boy wanted me to tell his mother something."

"What?"

"I don't know," I sniffed. "He couldn't get it out."

The copper wasn't so dumb after all. He snatched the handkerchief, looked into my eyes. Not a tear to show him. He shoved his face closer.

"Mother, hell! Come on, what'd he say? You're stalling! Want me to snatch you upstairs and get that mouth of yours working right?"

"Try it," says I, "and I'll start a backfire that'll blow you down the elevator shaft."

"I've heard plenty talk like that before."

But he twitched an eye toward the mayor. I knew what he was thinking. Here in the mayor's anteroom might mean I had an in after all. Sure enough. Out it came.

"What's your business here?"

"With His Honor."

"That isn't hard to guess. What kind of business?"

And I raised my voice again. "Listen, officer, are you trying to mix in the mayor's appointments? What business is it of yours whom the mayor sees? Are you trying to tell me my business with His Honor isn't important?"

The mayor heard it. So did the chief of police. So did everyone else in the room. I meant 'em to. And I followed it up by brushing past the copper to the mayor.

"Your Honor, do I have to stand there and be treated like a common criminal because I happened to be waiting for you at a time like this?"

Under my breath, without moving my lips, I spoke for his nearest ear only. "I'm Michael Harris, from the Blaine Agency."

Don't ever tell me a fat man can't think quick. His Honor caught it without batting a lid.

"Of course not, Harris!" he boomed indignantly. "I didn't know they were doing that to you!" He ignored the red-faced copper, swung on the chief. "Morgan, don't let your men be so blasted officious. It's ridiculous to think Harris knows anything about him. He doesn't even live in Middleton. He's an old—er—friend of the family."

"Sorry about it, Mr. Harris," the chief apologized. "I'll see it doesn't happen again."

A glint was in the chief's eye as he turned to the unhappy copper. And the mayor spoke solicitously:

"I'll see you now while we're waiting, Michael, my boy. Step into my office."

I walked out from under the noses of those coppers with the mayor's big arm about me. Which wasn't so bad at that.

3

BLACKMAIL

THE DOOR CLOSED. The mayor turned the latch, passed a handkerchief over his broad face as he walked to a desk between two tall windows. He was shaken, disturbed. Once more his hand was trembling as he took a bottle from a desk drawer and gulped from it without bothering to get a glass. Slapping the bottle down on the desk he glared at me.

"Let's see your credentials," he demanded curtly.

I showed him one pocket card I carried. We weren't encouraged to take even that out on a case. "If it isn't enough, there's a telephone to the New York office," I added.

He waved the suggestion aside.

"I didn't know there were two of you," he said.

"Parker sent for me. I just got in, telephoned him from the station and he said to come to your office. Just as he stepped into the doorway, someone fired into his back."

The mayor hoisted another drink. "Did you see who did it?"

"Just the tip of the gun. It was an automatic."

He had a third drink. His guard was down. He looked bad, was getting worse. Wagging his head dolefully, he said:

"Parker had something important to tell me. I wish I knew what it was."

"He had something on his mind," I said. "All he could get out was, 'Watch brunette…' Any sense to that?"

"Brunette? Brunette…" He shook his head. "Not a thing."

So I said: "What's it all about? What mess was Benny Parker digging into that would get him two bullets in the back? Hell, man, I never heard of anything like that. Right here under police headquarters; with cops crawling all over the place."

His Honor grabbed for the bottle the fourth time.

"It is a mess," he assented feverishly. "I didn't realize how much until this terrible thing happened. I—we'd better go out and see if they know who killed young Parker. I thought he was too young when he came, but he seemed to be making progress. If—if I can find out who shot him, I—I may get an idea."

I POUNDED THE desk corner, pulled a glare of my own.

"Maybe you won't get that idea," I told the mayor. "Benny Parker was a particular friend of mine. I don't know what brand of private hell you're having here. I don't give a damn! But if it isn't busted quickly, I'm in on it. What was Benny Parker doing here? And what's your name? I don't know that yet."

Me talk to the mayor like that? Sure. I'd faced 'em bigger than him. And he liked it. Brightening, he looked more at ease.

"When I called the Blaine Agency I wanted a man who could talk like that, Harris. I'm glad to hear it from you. My name is James L. Knapp. Did you notice this city hall?"

"Who could help it?"

Knapp put a palm on the desk blotter, leaned over, stared at me. His chin was bulgy, pendulous, but his cheeks were firm and healthy, and the nervousness dropped away from him as he spoke.

"Graft, Harris. This building cost too much. It's only one of many instances. For years they spent. New buildings, new streets, new everything."

"Civic spirit, eh?"

"Civic hell!" said the mayor violently. "Everything cost too much. The rake-off was tremendous. The men who ran this town ran it the way they pleased. They spent and kept on spending. When the money ran low they slapped on new taxes. Middleton is one of the highest-taxed places in the country."

"Ali Baba and his forty thieves must run the taxis," I growled.

"I see you've ridden in a local taxi. The high city license is responsible."

"Your policemen are snappy looking," I said.

"They should be," Knapp replied bitterly. "Their salaries are high enough. They may be worth it; I don't know. But I do know why they're getting it. Their pay was jacked up time after time so there could be no doubt who every man on the force was rooting for."

"Bought 'em, huh? I've seen it happen before."

Knapp tilted the bottle a fifth time, hardly noticing. He was too engrossed in what he was saying.

"I'm not blaming the police," he stated. "As far as I know they're a fair lot. But it's human to be for those who raise your pay and against those who want to cut it.

"I was elected for tax-reduction. I'm trying to do it. But a lot of the old crowd are still in. As soon as I started pruning I began to make enemies. I've cut police pay once and I'm going to do it again. What's the answer?"

"I'll bet they're not cheering for you," I guessed.

Knapp laughed shortly.

"I'm an enemy to every man on the force, except a few clear thinkers who realize it has to be done. A lot of people are out to get my scalp, quickly. The only way they can do that is to have me thrown out of the office in disgrace."

"You're still in," I said.

Knapp drew a long breath, opened the metal lid of a small cigarette chest on his desk, lighted a cigarette. Lines of worry, strain, were clearer on his face.

"I'm still in—but I don't know for how long. You see—I'm being blackmailed. That's why I retained the Blaine Agency."

IN THE ANTEROOM voices, movement, muffled confusion had not stopped. Someone tried the doorknob.

"I'm busy," Knapp called.

And I lowered my voice. "Blackmail, huh? Couldn't you handle it locally?"

Knapp laughed shortly again. "With a police force who hates my guts?" he countered, with human bluntness. "I hardly know who is for me and who is against me—but I'm damned sure the police aren't for me. Nor the papers. Any serious reflections against me would be in the next editions."

"I take it you've kept everything under cover so far then?"

"So far," Knapp agreed. But he looked bad as he said it. Fear, strain, hopelessness were in his voice and manner. "It's cost me a quarter of my capital so far," he told me heavily. "I can't keep up the drain much longer. And when I refuse to pay I'll be smeared all over the front pages at once. I know it. I'm merely waiting for it."

I guess I looked my disgust. Blackmail was a thing I hated worse than kidnaping and the people who paid blackmail rated pretty low with me. Ten to one if they came out and refused to pay that would be the end of it. Perhaps a little publicity, wiped off the papers and forgotten in no time. Most newspapers wouldn't even print the average stuff on which blackmail was based.

I told Knapp so.

He heard me out. His jaw was set, stubborn when I finished.

"You're right, Harris. I wouldn't pay a dollar, except to protect myself politically right now. I'm in here to do a job. I fought like hell to get in and I'm going to stay. I'm going to clean this town up, put it back on its feet, make such a splendid showing the old gang will never have a chance to get back in. It's a matter of pride. My great-grandfather was one of the first settlers here. All my money was made here. Most of it, anyway. Our plant—enameled kitchenware—is here."

Knapp's voice was low, hard, harsh with emotion. I forgot he was fat, forgot he was a small town mayor as he said:

"I'll pay to the last dollar if necessary to keep dirt off my name until I do this job right."

Hell, I was proud of that fat guy; proud to know him; proud there were men like him left to wade into politics with their sleeves rolled up. And when he said:

"I'm going to see that the man who shot Parker gets

everything the courts will hand out," I was for Knapp in a big way.

"BENNY PARKER WAS running down this blackmail angle?" I asked.

"Yes."

"Don't you know who's doing it?"

"I've never been able to find out. In my early twenties," said Knapp, "I was in San Francisco for several years gathering experience. The cashier of one firm I worked for embezzled heavily. His books were doctored. I had charge of some of them. Due to inexperience I didn't know what he was pulling off under my very nose. He was caught, killed himself, and I was left with the mess on my doorstep.

"The owner was crabbed and suspicious. He insisted I had knowledge of the matter, got some of his money. He pressed the charge. The facts were damaging. The loss was too great to ask my family to make up. No one knew who I was out there. Under my own name I served over a year in the penitentiary."

Knapp reached for the bottle a sixth time—and then let it stand there. His eyes were on me.

"No one in Middleton—not even my own family—knew what had happened," he said. "I came back here several years later, married and settled down. I thought the past was dead and buried. And then, three months after I was elected mayor, a man telephoned my house one evening, gave his name as Smith, and said he was collecting funds for a memorial to the members of the Knapp family."

Mayor Knapp snorted. "I told the fellow I wasn't interested. His manner was suave and a moment later he let the cat out of the bag by suggesting that when the fund was complete the records would be turned over to me, including finger-prints and all data concerning one of the Knapps who had served time in prison out West. He didn't need to say anything more. I knew what I was up against. I paid—ten thousand dollars the first time. If he had the records as he claimed, he kept them.

"It didn't matter. If they had not been stolen from the files, they could be checked easily enough. Since then," said Knapp, "I've paid steadily, about once a month. Different amounts. And I know when I'm bled dry the information will be sold to the highest bidder."

"But you've never seen the man?"

"Not once. He seems to know I'm helpless. I deposited the money in cash to an account called the Knapp Memorial Fund. It had already been opened. He was sure of me. B.L. Smith checks openly on the account for salaries and expenses, keeping it down to a few dollars. The checks are always cashed in other cities. I've never been able to get a line on him. I can't use the police. I'm afraid of any professional detectives from this section. So I called in the Blaine Agency."

"Why?"

"Because," said Knapp, "if this man Smith really has those records, I want them. And if he hasn't, when my job is through here in the mayor's office, I'm going to settle with him."

He looked hard, ugly, when he said that.

"Did Benny Parker find out anything at all?"

"Something," said Knapp. "He telephoned me this morning and said he wanted to see me this afternoon. He

intimated he had something important for me. That's all
I know."

"And when he came here with it, he was shot," I said.
"Sure it was important. Damned important. And there is
a woman connected with it. Will you call the hospital and
see how Benny is getting along?"

Knapp did that. His voice was thick when he hung up.

"Parker was dead before they got him out of the building here," he said.

You could feel the strain settle in that expensive office. I
felt haggard. Maybe I looked it. Knapp's eyes clung my face.

"It's murder now," I said.

"I can't condone murder," Knapp whispered. "I'll have
to tell the chief of police."

He started toward the door, and publicity, disgrace, and
the ruin of all his plans.

4

A DEAD MAN'S ROOM

I SAID: "WAIT a minute."

Knapp stopped, looking at me.

"How do you know this Smith had anything to do with shooting Parker?" I asked.

"That was all Parker was here for."

"Still—you don't know."

"Why argue about it? We both know."

"Let me look into it first," I said. "Maybe the police have got the man who did it. Maybe there's more to this than you think. Benny wouldn't have sent for me if he didn't need me. I know something no one else does. Benny kept a diary. Made his entries in it every night. It wouldn't be on him. Let me look at the diary first. Where did Benny stay?"

"I don't know," says Knapp.

But he looked like a drowning man who had grabbed at a straw which was keeping him up. He simply stood there, shoulders hunched down, waiting for me to do something.

So I said:

"Let's go out and see what the police are doing. Keep your mouth shut about me. I'm an old family friend, here in town for a visit. Not so hot for me, but the beans are spilled about it now. I'll get a hotel room and try to keep under cover."

"I'll do anything I can," Knapp promised, and he meant it. Then he rallied, walked to the door first, opened it. And His Honor preceded me into the anteroom.

We had been gone less than fifteen minutes. In that time the confusion had quieted, some of the coppers and plainclothesmen had cleared out, and the beefy chief of police had left.

All the visitors were there, nervous, ill at ease. The sharp featured woman who had pointed me out spoke indignantly.

"Mr. Mayor, how long do we have to stay here? I'm late for an appointment already."

"Not long, I hope, Mrs. Peabody," Knapp soothed her, and to one of the detectives he said: "Did they get the man who fired those shots?"

"Not yet, Your Honor."

"Where's Morgan?"

"Downstairs, I think, Your Honor."

The coppers might have hated his guts, but they were polite about it. Knapp took my arm.

"Let's go down and see what they're doing," he suggested.

So we went downstairs and found the chief of police standing inside the front doors, looking like a beefy bear spoiling for trouble.

Knapp addressed him curtly.

"What luck, Morgan?"

Unhappy? That big copper was in a sweat. "Nothing yet, Your Honor," says he reluctantly. "We're still holding everyone in the building, you see. But we're afraid the man escaped."

"Afraid?"

"We have his description," says the chief unhappily. "He was a tall, thin man. Two people on the second floor saw him running to the stairs after the shot. They didn't think quick enough to run after him. He ran to a patrolman on duty near the front door here, said there was trouble upstairs and he was going for a doctor."

"And the patrolman went upstairs and let the man go on out," I said.

The chief gave me a dirty took, bluffed to Knapp. "I've had a general alarm sent out for him. We'll have him shortly."

I shrugged, spoke to Knapp. "I might as well be going. I suppose it's all right, isn't it?"

"I don't see why not," says Knapp. "You have no objection to letting my—er—friend leave, have you, Chief?"

"Not if he's a friend of yours," says Morgan. But the way he looked at me I knew he'd like nothing better than to throw me in the tank for a week.

SO I LEFT, and paid sixty cents more to get back to the station and collect my bag. I was wondering if anyone would smell a rat and follow me. Apparently not. I took a room and bath at the Palace Hotel without spotting anyone at my heels.

The first thing I did was wire in code to Thompson, asking for a good woman to help me, reporting Benny's death, promising to keep the Agency out of it if possible.

Then I traced down Benny Parker's telephone number. It was a hotel. But what a hotel! A dump. A dive, down a

side street, next to an alley. The Century was the name, and
a good one. It must have been in that old red brick building
almost a century. Cheap hash joints, second hand stores,
and an auto wreckers' junk yard across the street at the next
corner set the tone for a shabby neighborhood stretching
north from that point.

A queer place for Benny Parker to hole up. But he must
have known what he was doing. And his diary evidently
was inside the place. A hock shop sold me a cheap, worn
suitcase; next door I got shoes, a suit and a hat to fit it; and
two hours after I had left the city hall I registered at the
Century Hotel as D. Jones, Chicago.

That was the tough side of an outside dick in a strange
town. A local man could have walked in there and searched
the room. I had to take a lot of trouble and risk to get the
same result without tipping my hand.

Risk? Wait till you hear. I didn't have any idea when I
waded through the garlic and old odors of the grimy little
lobby downstairs. The floor was covered with checked linoleum, worn to a smooth brown in many spots.

The desk had a tin top. The lobby chairs had cane seats.
The gaudy wall calendars were fly-specked and the front
windows had not been washed since the animals came out
of the ark.

The room cost me a dollar. The clerk walked me up to
the third floor himself—and let me carry my bag. A sign
in the hall said the bath was at the end of the hall, and the
floors creaked under each step.

The place was dim, dirty and depressing, and the over-
painted little zany who loitered in the hall at the head of

the stairs when I started down again drew a snort when she greeted me coyly.

"You're wasting your time, baby," I gave her. "I hate women. Beat it."

"You've got a nerve, you big palooka!" she called down the dark stairway after me.

"Thanks for the boost, kid," I sent back to her. "I'll have my heels raised an inch on that. You're the first nitwit who's called me big in six months."

THE USUAL SHABBY crew was loafing in the lobby. Down at the heels. Derelicts. Shabby. Some were smoking, reading. Two old gaffers were playing checkers over in the corner. A radio was blaring. Outside it was getting dark and someone was cooking liver and onions not far from the lobby.

I lit a cigarette and leaned an elbow on the tin counter in front of the dog-eared register.

"Jake Bernstein registered here yet?" I asked the clerk.

He was sallow, weedy and indifferent.

"Nope," he says. "Never heard of him."

"Kinda heavy fellow. Big lower lip. Black mustache. He's from Chi."

"I ain't seen him," the clerk yawned.

I was flipping absently back through the register as I talked. It wasn't hard. They didn't come and go fast in this joint. And I wasn't looking for Benny Parker's name. Chances were he hadn't used it here.

He hadn't. But there was his handwriting, clear, angular, bold. I'd seen a score of reports signed by it, read two brief notes Benny had sent me. Blond, grinning Benny Parker, who was on a slab now, cold and still.

It brought a lump to my throat, running across this trace of Benny. Benny Barton, he had called himself here. His room was 210, almost directly under mine.

"If Jake Bernstein registers," I said to the clerk, "tell him to come up to my room."

"Yeah," he agreed, inspecting the ends of his finger-nails. They needed cleaning.

The key to 210 was in the rack. I left it there, walked upstairs—and back along the second floor. A dim, dusty bulb cast sickly light. Under the strip of worn carpet the floor creaked softly. Room doors were like peeling fronts of cells.

The air reeked with poverty, despair, evil. Just that. I've seen it a thousand times. People leave something behind. How do we know exactly what a bloodhound follows?

Then—210—tin numerals tacked on the door, soiled china doorknob as Benny's hand had left it. I had my keys, those clever keys I'd collected to open any door. The second one turned the simple lock.

I opened the door, slipped into the dark room, fumbled for the light switch—and froze there as a gun slammed into my back.

5

MURDER'S TRAIL

I GRUNTED TOO. That gun muzzle almost cut me in two. A hand reached past my shoulder and closed the door. A key fumbled against the lock, slipped in, turned. We were locked in there together.

"I should have left the key in there."

You could have knocked me over with a whisper. A woman said that. Shakily. She was afraid, desperate, but she held that gun muzzle in my back like she was trying to poke it through the ribs.

"What's the idea, lady?" I said. "Is this the way to treat a guy when he comes into his room? If you want my dough, take all six dollars an' pull that rod outa me. I'm harmless."

She poked it in farther.

"I don't want your money," she said. "And you're lying. This isn't your room. Who are you?"

"Take it or leave it, I'm the night watchman, sister."

"That is a lie also."

Such correct English. Such delicate perfume. Such a controlled, modulated voice in spite of the tension gripping her. And I was right again about people having something you can feel in the air. She had it. She didn't belong here in this near flop house.

"What the devil are you doing in here?" I asked her.

She whispered fiercely: "Walk where I guide you! Keep quiet!"

Would you do it? I did. This woman wasn't trifling. Her gun trembled a little and that made it worse. She took me across the room, stopped me there, searched me.

She wasn't a good hand at frisking a man. But she got the keys from my hand, the automatic from under my arm. The six dollars I had brought along she left in my pocket.

So it wasn't theft after all.

"Sister," I asked, "are you a brunette?"

And she gasped a little and I knew I had hit it right. This must be the woman Benny had tried to tell me about. I hated her then. She must have some connection with the rat who had killed Benny. If it hadn't been for the gun in my back—

She pushed me into a clothes closet, shut the door, locked it. The key had already been in the lock. It turned as I grabbed the knob and lunged against the door. Three seconds later and I'd have been out at her, taking my chances on missing her in the dark.

She didn't laugh, didn't speak. In the cramped closet, with coat hangers jingling about my head, I listened, heard no further sounds from her.

After several minutes of that I sat down on the floor, back against the wall, feet against the bottom of the door, and pushed until the lock cracked loudly and the door flew open.

Old cheap doors can be handled like that. It made plenty of noise. The sound was still in my ears as I felt my way to the door and snapped on the light.

One look at Benny's room and I really damned her. Everything had been searched. Benny's suitcase was open, contents strewn on the floor. Bureau drawers had been pulled out, bed covers pulled back, pillows tumbled about.

No use looking for Benny's diary in here. To make sure I pawed through the contents of his battered traveling bag. It was the one he'd always carried. Often I had seen Benny slip the leather bound diary in the side pocket. It was gone now.

And as I stood up I heard heavy steps leave the stairs and come along the hall. Back to the door; off with the light in case someone would notice it through the keyhole.

Two sets of steps creaked along the hall. And stopped at the door. A key scraped and the door opened.

I DIDN'T HAVE a chance to hide, I couldn't have done so if there had been time. There wasn't even a bath to the room. The clothes closet with its splintered door was worse than nothing. Also one set of those steps had tramped with the stolid certainty of authority.

Sure, if it wasn't one thing it was another. A copper was outside and I was trapped in Benny's room on as sweet a charge of breaking and entering as one could figure out. I just had time to draw back into the shadows as the door opened.

I saw him first against the hall light, that square-faced, ponderous dick who had tried to crack down on me in the Mayor's office. He had me this time. It would be duck soup for him. Mike Harris, the red-headed wonder, had balled the case up toot-sweet now.

I swung my fist from the floor as he stepped through the doorway.

Smash! The jolt shook me to my heels, numbed my fist. But square on the side of the jaw it caught him as sweet a clip as I've ever seen. That big copper never knew what happened. He floated back on his heels and tumbled into the man standing behind him.

I caught one glimpse of the weedy clerk as he went down under the copper's weight. Squawking bloody murder as they tumbled on the floor.

The door was shut by then. Two jumps took me across the room. The window was locked. I found the catch, snapped it over. The clerk's feet thudded along the hall, down the stairs. His yells for the police were still audible as I wiped the window latch with my handkerchief and shoved the window up.

The copper's hand had mussed any prints I had left on the doorknob. I was in the clear on the closet door. The clerk hadn't had a chance to spot me. Snatching a sheet, I draped it over the window sill to hide any chance of a print, slid out, hung down as far as I could and dropped.

The alley was down there. No cars were under me. The pavement was old brick. I'd done this sort of thing before, but the shock was pretty bad at that. My feet were half numb as I staggered back into the cloaking darkness of the alley.

I think I'd have tried to get up to my room by the back way if it hadn't been for the copper. They'd search the hotel now. It wouldn't do me any good to be found there under another name.

So I made the next street, cut back to the main street, lost myself in the crowd. I was mad. Everything was balled up. Maybe I'd be traced by the suitcase in my room, by the clerk's description when they found my room empty. And a woman had made a fool of me and walked off as calmly as a possum from a hen roost. The one woman in town I wanted, too.

What next? The Palace Hotel first, to turn back into Mike Harris.

I did that, made a bundle out of my old clothes, carried them out and ditched them in a side street sewer and hoped for the best. That big dick would be snorting for blood from now on.

THEN I HAD a brainstorm and telephoned Thompson in New York. It took the telephone people half an hour to locate him, and when Thompson heard what I wanted he turned me down flat.

"Can't be done tonight, Harris."

"It better be. I'm sitting on a hot pot here and the lid's ready to blow."

"Let it blow," Thompson rasped. "Have you found out who killed Benny Parker?"

"I'm trying to. This is part of it. Will you give me some action?"

"I'll give you anything you want," Thompson came back in a near snarl, "but you get the man who killed Parker. Has Trixie Meehan got there yet?"

And I yelped then.

"Did you send Trixie Meehan here to help me?"

"She should be there any minute," Thompson says frostily. "And if the two of you get in another fight I'll fire you both. I'm getting damn sick of the feud between you two."

He slammed up the receiver.

I slammed up mine. Trixie Meehan again. She dogged

my life. I couldn't get away from her. And all because she was smart and I was supposed to be smart and luck gave the two of us a break now and then. But Trixie was giving me gray hairs.

Then I forgot Trixie as I steamed up to the Palace Hotel marquee. Yeah, I had walked down to another hotel to make my call to Thompson. There getting into a taxi in front of the hotel was a woman. Three girls crowded me to the curb and I heard her tell the driver:

"Jack's place."

A whiff of delicate perfume, a voice I couldn't mistake, and as the taxi rolled away I beckoned the next one up.

"Jack's place, quick!" I said.

Behind us an automobile horn blew violently. A woman in a big, sleek coupé was trying to get to the marquee. I had to jump in and repeat my order; then the hacker took me away from there in a rush. And I sat back in the seat and lit a cigarette with shaking hands. I didn't know where Jack's place was. Didn't care. It was enough that the dame heading there was the one who had stuck a gun in my back in Benny's room.

6

AT JACK'S PLACE

THAT MODULATED VOICE of hers was a dead giveaway and she had trailed the same perfume into the taxi. She was going places now. Jack's place was out of town, a huge, one-storied log structure, spangled with light in front, ringed with cars, filled with life inside.

I'd seen its kind before outside of small towns and big ones. Places where the food was good, the dancing ditto, and any hell a little freer than in town under the eyes of the cops. Nothing vicious perhaps; just the big, expansive open places.

By the number of cars parked outside, the best people in town came here. By the number of well-dressed people I spotted inside, there was no doubt of it.

We were minutes ahead of the other car. A chic checkroom-girl took my hat. A black-coated headwaiter bowed suavely. "One, sir?"

"One," I said, looking past him at the big low-ceilinged room filled with tables, with diners, with couples already dancing.

I drew a table near the rear of the room, back from the dance floor. It suited me. I could see the entrance to the

room. A waiter came up. I ordered a steak, shoestring pota-
toes, sliced tomatoes and a sloe gin rickey.

She came in before I got my drink. I spotted her by her
hat. I think I'd have known her by her walk. It matched her
voice. Easy, controlled, every movement right and perfect.

She was a silver brunette, dark hair, light dainty complex-
ion, trim, trig, pretty and smart. Her mouth was small; her
face just a little long; her small hat had a saucy veil down
over her eyes, and she was about twenty-three.

The headwaiter scraped the floor. She tossed him a smile,
walked past him to the aisle on the other side of the dance
floor. Halfway back she turned into a low-arched doorway
and vanished.

So I knew she was a regular here. She hadn't come to eat.
And if my guess was only worth half as much as I thought
it was, she carried a rod in the pocketbook tucked under
her arm.

And there I was with a steak coming up, a drink half
down. A crooner did his stuff through a megaphone.
People drifted in and out through that parched doorway
across the room. And I left my table and went to see what
lay beyond that arch.

I might have known. Gambling. Food, dancing and
a bum floor show couldn't have dragged all these smart
people out here often enough to keep the place going.

At least half the crowd was in there at the tables.
Roulette and dice were the main games. The play wasn't
high. Probably it would be jacked up later in the evening
when the hot shots got going.

And I looked for my lady—and looked and looked. She
wasn't at the tables.

THEN IN ONE corner of the room a door opened and she came out, followed by a man; What a swell-looking couple they made. He was a head taller, square-shouldered, slim-hipped. His hair was black also. His carefully trimmed little mustache balanced the only defect I could spot in that brief look.

His mouth was a trifle small, a bit too weak, a shade too selfish and cruel. But you had to look close to see that. He was too handsome; his walk was even more distinctive than hers—smooth, gliding, pantherish.

Nope, I wasn't getting poetic—but they had come through a doorway marked MANAGER'S OFFICE and I gave him the eye hard. I might want to know him the next time we met.

Nudging a young fellow next to me who looked like a regular, I asked:

"Is that the manager?"

He followed the jerk of my head.

"Yeah," he said. "And owner too, I guess. That's Jack DeLand. He's been the big shot around here ever since it opened last spring."

"Thanks," I said. "I just wondered. Who's the girl?"

"Search me," he said; "Never saw her before. They're all after him."

"Ladies' man, eh?"

"Nope," says my young fellow with a cigarette hanging from his lower lip and his hat on the back of his head. "He laughs it off an' lets 'em alone."

"Middleton must be a live town."

"You can get action," he said, and turned back to watch the dice game.

And I drifted across to the manager's office and stepped inside. Why? Well, she had gone in there with her purse and come out without it. And I had a hunch that one look in that purse might be useful to Mike Harris, the old maestro.

It was another tight corner. I didn't have any business in that office. I went in ready to back out with an idle excuse, and found it empty and went to work quickly.

A couple of filing cases, a table and typewriter, a desk, book shelves and easy leather chairs and a deep rug on the floor made it a snug little nook. The dainty fragrance of her presence still lingered in the air.

And there was her purse on the corner of the desk.

Inside I found the rod, mother-of-pearl inlaid, short barreled, thirty-two caliber, nasty and deadly. And a roll of bills, a little morocco bound address book, several cards, handkerchief, chased silver compact and a lipstick.

Benny Parker's diary was not there.

I TOOK THE address book, one of the cards—and a moment later dove behind the desk with the whole purse as the door opened. It was a mess this time. Maybe I could have bluffed it out, but I wanted that address book in my pocket. I didn't want to be questioned, perhaps searched.

And they came in, two men. The door closed. Under the desk I could see the legs of one as he moved to the center of the room. The little thirty-two automatic was in my hand now. I was going to have to bluff with it. Another minute and he'd discover me—

But he stopped there, turned his heels to me, spoke in a husky, whining voice. "What's the idea of telling me to come in here like this?"

The other's voice was clipped, brusque.

"I borrowed DeLand's office so no one could hear us or get a look at your face while I talk to you."

"What's wrong with my face? I'll bite. What's on your mind, Slim?"

"You," said Slim. I couldn't see him, but his voice was ugly. "You rat," Slim said. "You damned, double-crossing rat! We've just been tipped off what you've been up to."

"I don't know what you mean, Slim."

The whine was still in that husky voice. No anger, in spite of the names that had been called. I couldn't see them, but I could feel them looking at each other.

Hell was in the air, if you get what I mean. My right leg was cramped under me until it hurt, and I forgot all about it. Something was going to happen. I couldn't figure what.

Slim said: "A dick was killed this afternoon on the second floor of the city hall. Right in the doorway of the mayor's office."

"Why tell me about that, Slim. I read the papers. Everyone's talking about it. Only none of it says he was a dick."

"He was."

"How do you know?"

"He left a diary in his room," Slim said curtly. "In it he put down who he was dealing with."

The man with his heels turned to me thought that over for a minute. His voice sounded strained when he spoke.

"Interesting. I'd like to see that diary. Got it here, Slim?"

"No," Slim said. "You wouldn't get your crooked hands on it if it was here. But your name was in it. You're through here in town, Kennedy. You've got until morning to lam."

"And leave everything here?"

"You heard me."

Kennedy thought that over too. "Who was that woman DeLand was with a few minutes ago?"

"None of your business."

Kennedy said: "I don't get a break then?" His voice was quiet now, not so husky. But I wanted to yell. I think I knew then what was coming.

"You a break?" Slim laughed. It was nasty, that laugh. "Eight o'clock tomorrow morning is all the break you get," he said.

Kennedy was silent again.

The room held the quiet of death. It must have been sound-proofed, because the noise in the gambling room was shut out. Slim's startled oath, a quick movement were the first things I heard. Then the shot—and a body thudding on the floor—and Kennedy's quick move—and the light went out.

12

TRIXIE CUTS A CORNER

I THOUGHT KENNEDY would run out the door. But a bolt
clicked hard and he came charging back toward the desk
where I stood in the darkness.

He was swearing under his breath. He couldn't see me,
didn't know I was there as he struggled to open the window
at one side of the desk.

A fist hammered on the door.

"What's wrong in there?" a muffled voice called sharply.

Kennedy didn't answer.

I jumped to him, jabbed the little automatic against him.
"Hold it!" I gave him cold. "It's an arrest!"

He whirled. I think he was crazy in that moment; crazy
with fear, desperation. I felt him grabbing for his pocket;
I knew what he was going to do—and I pulled the trigger
of the automatic to save myself.

The firing pin clicked on an empty breech. I pulled the
slide back, squeezed the trigger again—and got a second
empty click; and jumped aside with that empty, useless gun
as Kennedy's elbow caught me across the eyes and his gun
barked once more.

Through coat, shirt, to my skin that searing blast drove.

Stumbling back before it my foot caught the edge of the desk and I sprawled back heavily.

He must have thought me dead. With a chair he smashed the window out, and scrambled through as I staggered to my feet. They were trying to break the door in now. It was no place for Mike Harris. I faded through that broken window also.

The night air felt cool, clean. I was at the back corner of one wing. The lights were out in front. Kennedy's steps were pounding that way. I followed.

He got there well ahead of me. I glimpsed him leaping into a parked sedan. The motor started, the car lurched forward, kicking gravel back, and shot to the road in gear.

And over at my left a horn blew sharply. A voice called: "Mike! Over here!"

I thought I was delirious then. That was Trixie's voice. Trixie Meehan, who had no business out here, who couldn't be here in a car—and who was.

She had the sleek, powerful coupé rolling as I lunged in beside her.

"FOLLOW THAT CAR!" I gasped.

She did, taking the turn into the highway on two wheels. It must have done the same on one wheel, for it was already far down the road toward town.

"Well, Ape," says Trixie, "I see you've managed to get yourself into trouble right away. What happened?"

Cool and sarcastic. She hunched behind the wheel like a pert little French doll. Innocent, sweet and helpless. That was Trixie Meehan when you looked at her. She'd taken many a man for a ride on the strength of it. For Trixie was the hottest woman operative on the Blaine Agency list.

Her mind had been honed on a razor stone, her nerve dipped in a steel bath. She could out-think, out-work and get more results than most men.

And how Trixie did ride me every chance she got.

"Plenty happened!" I snapped bitterly. "I think a man has just been murdered back there. I was in the room with him. The fellow who did it threw a shot at me, busted out the window and scrammed. That's him ahead. I don't know whether I'm wounded or not."

Trixie spoke anxiously, without taking her eyes off the road over which we were streaking.

"Mike, are you hurt?"

I felt myself. Found no blood.

"Guess not," I said.

"Too dumb," says Trixie. "Who killed who and why? What were you doing there?"

"Checking up on a woman."

"You would be," says Trixie. "Her husband catch you?"

"Dumb-bell. This thing is hot. Benny Parker got killed on it. And then Thompson," I said bitterly, "had to inflict *you* on me. What were you doing out there in front of Jack's? Where did you get this car?"

"Bought it," Trixie said pertly. "And drove down from New York in it this evening. I pulled up in front of the hotel just as you were scrambling into a taxi. I blew my horn and you didn't pay any attention. So I followed to see what you were up to. I was waiting out in front for you when you came leaping along like a dog with a can on his tail."

"Look *out!*" I yelled as Trixie wrenched the wheel, slammed on the brakes and skidded around a farm wagon that had no lights. My hair was standing up straight as she put the speedometer up above sixty-five again.

"I saw it," says Trixie sweetly. "Don't be a baby, Mike. Look how fast that man ahead is going."

He was doing better time than we were. Trixie rocketed around a curve just in time to catch his tail lights vanishing off the road to the right.

"Got a gun?" I asked feverishly.

"In the dash compartment."

I felt better with a thirty-eight automatic in my hand. And just as I did Trixie slammed on the brakes again and skidded into that side road. I thought the tires were coming off, the car going over as we went clear to the edge of the road.

Some way Trixie got us out of it in a series of drunken lurches. I could hardly speak.

"If I get out of this alive, I'll never step in another car with you, s'help me!" I croaked.

Trixie giggled.

"All you need is a little self control, Mike. Do you think he'll shoot if we catch up with him?"

"Shoot? He'd cut loose with a machine gun if he had one. Maybe he has."

"Wouldn't that be ducky?" says Trixie, and peeled off the surface of the dirt road as she slid around the next corner.

It was so bad by then I didn't know who was going to kill me first, Trixie or the unknown Kennedy ahead. She could have been pinched for attempted assault with a deadly car. SEVERAL MILES FURTHER on he turned left again, toward town once more. I'd figured he was doing that;

coming in by another way in case a quick telephone call from Jack's place had the highway blocked.

"What will we do if we catch him?" Trixie asked.

"Turn him over to the cops."

"And suppose he swears you did that shooting? Were there any witnesses?"

I groaned. "Why bring that up? I should have stayed and faced it out and I didn't dare to. My hat's back there in the checkroom, my dinner's waiting on the table. There's a regular who can connect me with the office where the killing occurred and they'll have my description down pat."

"Poor Mike," says Trixie with all the enthusiasm of a wake.

"Lay off that. I'll take a rap if I have to. That bird ahead knows who killed Benny Parker. Maybe he did it himself. I'm going to get him."

"Maybe," says Trixie, and tires shrieked again as she skidded around a corner under an electric light. We were on the outskirts of town now. This Kennedy was doubling and eeling through badly lighted streets like a dancer going through a crowded floor.

And then—

One turn he was there; the next he wasn't. He had streaked up an alley, made a second turn too quick for us; anyway he was gone.

"Back to the hotel," I said. "I'm expecting a wire from Thompson."

"You'll get worse than a wire if this sort of thing keeps up," Trixie sniffed. "Does this town have radio police cars?"

"It does."

Trixie fiddled with a dial on the dash, got this station and that, and suddenly loud and clear a local station.

"…reported entering city at high speed on Grady Road. Search all suspicious cars."

Trixie drove slower. "I wonder if they've got your description, Mike."

"If they haven't, someone is dumb. Wait near the hotel door while I hop in and see if that wire has come."

It was still early in the evening. The lobby of the Palace was filled with activity. A casual glance was all I got from the desk clerk as he handed me a telegram and my room key.

I started to toss the key back, thought better and turned to the elevator. Two couples stepped in ahead of me. As the door closed I looked back into the lobby—and almost ducked. That big dick I had punched on the jaw was ploughing toward the desk; and he looked hard and businesslike.

"Mezzanine," I said, forgetting all about my room.

From behind a mezzanine pillar I looked down into the lobby at the desk. The big dick was talking to the clerk, and the clerk was nodding and pointing toward the elevators. The copper made for them—and I made for the stairs and faded through a corner of the lobby and out through the door as he started up.

13

A KEY TO THE TRAIL

TRIXIE SAID: "IT must have been *some* wire to put you in a sweat like this."

"Get going," I told her. "I'm on a spot. A copper is up at my room now trying to corner me. He's looking for trouble too. I smacked him on the jaw earlier in the evening,"

"Is there anything you haven't done since you've been in town?" Trixie gasped. "Of all the dumb stunts, trying to beat up a cop."

"Lay off," I snarled. "Stop at the first drug store."

She did. I hopped in, looked into a telephone directory, got some directions from the man behind the cigar counter and gave them to Trixie.

"Now listen," I said as we drove off. "When you let me out, get back to the hotel as quick as you can and register. Then drive out to Jack's place, order a sandwich, and pick up all the dope you can. Keep your eyes peeled for Jack DeLand, the owner, and a woman he was talking to the last time I saw him."

I described them.

"Then," I finished, "use your own judgment. If they're there and look like tailing will do some good, do it. If not, get back to the hotel and wait for a telephone call."

"And you?" says Trixie.

"If I knew, I'd be good enough to hang out my shingle as a fortune teller."

We found the address I was looking for. Trixie drove off and I walked past shrubbery and trees to an oldish, dignified brick mansion.

A servant answered the door. I gave him my name; and he closed the door and locked it while he announced me. A few moments later Mayor Knapp himself opened the door in person.

"Well, Harris, have you got something for me?" he beamed.

"You'd be surprised," I told him, walking in. "I've come to stay while your police try to scratch me out of their hair."

He changed color, stopped smiling, stared uncertainly. "What's that?"

"A man was shot out at Jack's roadhouse this evening. I'm afraid I'm connected with it. Your police are after me, anyway."

Knapp reddened. "Do you mean you're in trouble already and running to me for protection? Expecting me to shelter a fugitive?"

I grinned; he looked too sick and angry.

"That's right," I said. "What better place to hide than in the mayor's house?"

"By heavens, you'll not hide here!" Knapp exploded. "You're discharged from the case! I'll notify the Blaine Agency and handle this myself!"

So I stopped grinning and talked turkey.

"Like hell you will!" I told the mayor of Middleton. "I'm sticking until I get a break. Don't blame me if your police have got their wires crossed. I'm going to grab the rat who killed Parker, and clean up your mess while I'm doing it. Maybe I won't be quick enough to shut off talk, but I'll land the guy who's bleeding you."

"Don't take that tone with me!" Knapp choked.

"Nuts!" I said. "Take me to a quiet place where we can talk. I've got work to do."

HE WANTED TO throw me out. I was suddenly only trouble in his soup. I don't think he knew why he did it; obviously against his will he led the way into a library lined with books from floor to ceiling. Women's voices were audible until he closed a door at the back of the room. His eyes were haunted again as he turned to me.

"My wife and daughters," he said. "They'll suffer if this gets out. And I warn you, I'll not help you break the law."

"Who said anything about breaking it? The worst we'll do is strain it a bit."

Sure I felt sorry for him. How could I help it? Now I couldn't even promise him his record wouldn't get out. Murder inquiries can turn up a lot of dirt.

On a dark walnut table I'd tossed the soft leather purse and empty automatic. Knapp eyed them suspiciously. "Whose are those?"

"Souvenirs." Leafing through the little leather-bound address book, I whistled softly. "Somebody has been up in the gilt."

"What's that?"

"Here's the address of the daughter of a former cabinet member. And here's the name of Jerry Van Lander, of San Francisco. I'll bet it's the banking Van Landers."

"Never heard of them," Knapp said impatiently. "What are you driving at, Harris?"

I didn't know myself. That little address book was a gold mine of names, addresses and telephone numbers, scattered from one end to the other, with the majority out on the coast.

Enough of the names belonged to wealthy, influential families to suppose that the whole list was gilt-edged.

But nary an entry to suggest the name and address of the young woman who owned the book. Then, near the back, I found a new list, a later list, containing thirty or forty names. Then I did whistle softly, looking sideways at Knapp.

"Who's Jessica Knapp?" I asked.

"My oldest daughter," he snapped. "Why?"

"And who is Mrs. Byron Case?"

"She is the wife of the owner of the afternoon paper. He fought my election tooth and nail. Look here, Harris, what's all this leading up to?"

"Have a look at these names."

He did, looking bewildered. "These are Middleton people. Our best families. Mrs. Clyde Hunter... Mrs. Gordon Merrick Jr.... Mrs. Sam Walters Jr.... Miss May Lewis... Miss Caroline Holmes—

"These are all members of my daughter's set," Knapp stated when he finished the list. "What does it mean?"

So I said: "Call your daughter and ask her."

He stepped to that door he had closed; called: "Jessica."

WHILE WE WAITED I read the telegram Thompson had sent. Then I felt better. A hunch I'd had had been right. Shoving it in my pocket I faced Jessica Knapp as she came in. Nineteen or twenty, tall, willowy, smart, she looked like a product of an eastern finishing school. Very finished. She was politely curious as Knapp introduced her. He said:

"Jessica, does this list of names have any meaning to you? Your name is included."

She looked, bit her lower lip, breathed a little faster as she read. She had control, but not enough. Those names upset her. Her eyes went to me when she finished, and her question startled even me.

"Is this man a detective?" she asked.

"Uhhh—that has nothing to do with it," Knapp stalled.

"I don't know anything about this list," she said, handing it back to him. She was lying and Knapp knew she was lying as well as I did.

He reddened, said: "I'll see you alone for a moment, Jessica."

And he took her out of the room. It was more than a minute, ten, perhaps, before he returned. I'd heard his distant voice raised in anger. He was pale, shaken, when he returned: He wiped his face with a trembling hand.

"I'll have her raided and dragged into court!" he seethed. "If they can't sentence her, I'll see that she's run out of town!"

"Bravo!" says I. "You're not talking about your daughter, I hope."

Before Knapp could answer me the library door opened and the manservant looked in.

"The chief of police and another gentleman are here, sir," he announced.

9

GAMBLERS' HEAVEN

AND THERE I was.

Knapp choked, forgot his anger, looked at his man, at me, and didn't know what to do. I could see he thought all the dirt had washed-up on his doorstep now. Behind me was a curtained alcove. I looked in, saw it would hold me and grinned at Knapp.

"Have them in," I said.

He swallowed, passed the order along. I was behind the curtains out of sight when the men were shown in. The beefy chief of coppers came to the point at once; if subtle triumph wasn't in his voice, I was getting twisted ears.

"Your Honor," he says, "can you tell us where this young friend of yours is? This Mr. Harris?"

Knapp waited so long before replying that I started to sweat. He was primed to turn me in. It might seem the best way—and then the trouble would start. But he said:

"Did you come out here just to ask me that, Morgan? Haven't you a telephone?"

I thought I'd better talk to you personally," said the other. "We're looking for your friend, Mr. Harris, on suspicion of assaulting an officer, and murder."

Knapp managed surprise. "You must be wrong, Morgan."

"Not a chance," said the chief doggedly—and he told Knapp how they'd gotten my description at the Century and at Jack's. I'd been seen going into the office at Jack's.

Knapp said: "Are you trying to tell me Harris registered at two hotels, and then stepped out of another man's dark room and knocked this big detective unconscious? This man is twice as big as Harris."

Through a slit in the curtains the big copper I had slammed looked like thirty cents. The chief's "Murphy wasn't looking for it," didn't make him look any better. The chief went on doggedly:

"But it's the roadhouse matter we want Harris for. Slim Smith, the dead man, held a deputy's commission from the sheriff's office. He was paid by DeLand to keep order around the place. The sheriff has put it up to me to get the killer if he's in town—and I think he is. Harris was seen going into that office a little while before the murder."

"Sure of that?" Knapp snapped.

"Someone who looked like him, anyway. Red hair and all. This party left his hat in the checkroom and his dinner on the table uneaten when he went out that broken window. We want Harris for questioning and identification."

Knapp was in it now over his ears. His next remark put his head under.

"You'll be saying next that Harris may be around the house here."

"No, sir," the chief denied. "I just wanted to let you know. It's all right, I suppose, to pick Harris up?"

"Why not?" Knapp snapped. "You're running the department. Is that all?"

"Yes, sir."

"Good night."

THEY LEFT. I eased out into the room. Knapp was fingering his jaw. He looked half sick with worry again.

"I'm ruined already," he groaned. "I ought to kick you out and call the police. Morgan is a holdover from the old administration. He thinks he's got something on me and he's pressing it hard. Damn you, Harris!"

"Hold it in a little longer," I said. "What were you talking about when those men were announced?"

"That Chase woman!"

"What Chase woman?" And I felt my break was coming at last. Lord knew I needed it.

Knapp talked, scowling.

"Mrs. Chase is a divorcee whom my daughter met quite casually some months ago. Jessica introduced her to most of the people on that list. It seems that the Chase woman has turned her smart apartment into a gambling den. No men are allowed. The younger set from our best families, married and unmarried, frequent the place now. Gambling has become reckless and for high stakes. Those who win are paid promptly, and those who lose can sign for it."

"Who finally pays for them?"

"I don't know," Knapp said grimly. "Jessica owes the woman over a thousand dollars and no attempt has been made to collect."

I was grinning. I couldn't help it. The break was getting better.

"I'd like to talk to your daughter," I said.

Knapp got her. She had been crying. She faced me sullenly.

"When do your friends go to Mrs. Chase's apartment?" I asked her.

"Any time from noon to midnight," she replied sullenly. "And—and don't either of you dare to humiliate me before the whole town. I'm old enough to know what I'm doing."

Knapp snorted angrily.

"The place has become a club of sorts, Harris," he said. "A French maid has charge when the Chase woman is out. It's probably crowded tonight. I'll have it raided at once, no matter what the consequences are."

"Not so fast. I've got a better idea. Miss Knapp, tell me everything about the apartment that you can remember."

She refused to talk until her father ordered it; then did so unwillingly. But when she was through I had a clear picture of the place, who went there, what the routine was. And I let her go and floored Knapp with my next request.

"I want to telephone San Francisco."

"I think you're insane," Knapp said. "But I'm nearly so. There's the telephone."

I called our San Francisco office, got Billy Knibbs, who was just starting out to his house.

"Get in touch with the best newspaper morgue in town and get the dope on the love tangles of Charles Sands," I told Billy. "Telephone it back to me as quickly as you can."

Billy's yelp was anguished across three thousand miles of wire.

"I'm just starting home to change my clothes!" he moaned. "I've got a date I worked months to get. I can't stand her up. You guys there in the East are crazy!"

"It's the love life of Charles Sands I'm after; not yours," I told Billy. "And I'm in a hurry for it."

CUTTING OFF ANOTHER moan, I called Trixie's room. She was not in. So I said to Knapp:

"Who's Kennedy?"

"Who?"

"A chap named Kennedy. I don't know his first name."

Knapp wrinkled his forehead. "I know several Kennedys. The Reverend Abel Kennedy—"

"Hardly the one."

"Dr. James Kennedy, one of our best surgeons."

"I doubt it."

"There's a head bookkeeper in the city treasurer's office; a detective on the homicide squad; a garage owner seven blocks down this street; a jeweler down town; a politician in the third ward; a vice-president of one of the banks—"

I waved him down. "Too many to do me any good. Haven't got time to look them all up. I think I can locate him."

Knapp was getting in a dither; "What are you going to do, Harris?"

"Leave you," I said. "Keep this address book and purse. If I get pinched, I'll send you word."

"Don't you dare carry this miserable farce to that length, Harris!"

But I was calling Trixie again. Still out. Billy Knibbs telephoned back, talked four minutes without a stop, and hung up and raced for his date. Trixie answered the next time I asked for her. Her first crack was:

"You're famous, Mike. The place was crowded. Everyone was talking about you."

"I'll bet. Did you see the woman?"

"Not a glimpse; or the man either."

"Come get me and bring your artillery." Before I left the house I warned Knapp. "No telephoning for your daughter tonight."

He nodded, asked dry-lipped, for the umptieth time: "What are you going to do, Harris?"

"Start the razzle-dazzle," was all the comfort I gave him.

Trixie picked me up at the curb, spun me through streets faster than I cared to go. She was a maniac at that wheel. I talked fast, telling her what to do.

Trixie razzed me. "Your midget brain must have worked hard to think that out, Mike. Trying to get me killed, too?"

"Backing out?"

"Hah!" says Trixie. *"Me* back out? Dry your tears with an onion!"

So we squabbled for another half mile, and Trixie let me out at a street corner. As I closed the car door I weakened.

"Watch yourself, kid," I said gruffly. "Two dead ones are enough in this mess."

"Worried about me, Mike?" Trixie asked, suddenly tender.

"Hell, no. But I need you alive, not dead."

Sore about something, Trixie spun her rear wheels and shot down the street; and I followed her into the next block and entered a swanky apartment house some minutes after her.

10

SECRET OF THE BOX

FOR A TOWN the size of Middleton that apartment house was hot. Ten stories high, two elevators, a doorman in charge of the lobby who would have made three of me. He looked like an overgrown plug-ugly and he should have been bouncing beer bums in a waterfront saloon. But his voice had been filed down smoothly and he had learned English somewhere.

"Yes, sir," he said, slipping me a frosted smile. "Who do you wish to see?"

"Mrs. Chase's apartment."

He froze. "Impossible. Mrs. Chase does not receive men."

"My wife just went up. I saw her turn the corner down the street a few minutes ago. We're to meet at Mrs. Chase's." And I described Trixie briefly.

He was stumped.

"Your name, please?" he asked. And he telephoned the apartment, announced me, listened, hung up. "Ninth floor," he said. And he still looked dazed when the elevator whisked me up.

I had the layout. Mrs. Chase occupied the whole ninth floor. She had spread out, remodeled with the rush of business. Only part of the floor was occupied, but she had privacy.

From the elevator I stepped into a spacious, chummy reception room. Just like home. But the chairs and couches were never used. The door at the left was the entrance. It was always opened first on a chain by the smart French maid. She had to know you before you got in. The gatherings inside were strictly hand picked and safe. If you got past the Cossack downstairs—who was paid by Mrs. Chase—and the elevator boys, you still were on the outside. Trixie was the only one who could have made the grade, and she had to do it alone.

But Trixie had gone over the top with a bang. That telephone call was proof of it. I knocked on the door confidently. It opened and I walked in, saying:

"Baby, you sure handled that neat."

"Didn't I?" says Trixie. "Mabel, meet the boy friend."

Mabel hissed: "Peeg!"

Mabel's hands were in the air and her white lace cap was askew. A bit angular and hard-faced, Mabel was plain mad now as she stood there with Trixie's gun in her back.

"I had to weep," Trixie giggled. "She wasn't going to open the door until I said Jessica, dear Jessica Knapp, was coming to meet me here in a few minutes. They're all gone, Mike. No one here but Mabel."

"My name ees not Mabel!" the maid frothed.

"It's mud now," Trixie gave her cheerfully. "She won't talk, Mike. Not a word."

"**HOLD HER QUIET** while I look around," I said, locking the door.

And what followed was the quickest frisk I had ever

given a place. Some place too. First a huge, softly lighted room which would have made a sultan's harem swoon with envy. Soft scents, soft lights, soft couches and chairs, dainty and fragile, it was a hen's paradise. No wonder the girls with time on their hands had made this their hangout.

Bridge tables, bridge lamps, a nifty little roulette layout, a dainty dice table—it was Jack's place gone feminine. Bedrooms to match, private rooms with tables and chairs in them; and at the bottom of a large bureau in the niftiest bedroom of all I turned up a small locked tin box.

I suppose the place didn't have a wall safe and she hadn't bothered to have one put in. I never saw a woman yet who didn't think her bureau drawers had magic to hold her valuables. It took me about three minutes to get past the lock of that box and lift the lid.

It was jammed with papers. No money. But what papers. Enough to fill an iceman's fist. What the Chase woman had done to the wives and daughters with her perfumed gambling hell was enough to gag a banker. The girls had lost plenty, and had signed; and were doubtless wiggling and squirming now and wondering what to do about it.

And then down near the bottom I let out a whoop. Prison papers, fingerprint cards, prison photos, dates years old; the picture and history of all that Knapp had told me down there in black and white. An opposition newspaper would cry tears of joy to get their hands on this proof.

And Benny Parker's diary was there. I put it aside for a moment, opened another notebook. Smiles on the Great Stone Face! Here was the dirt of the town, all put down meticulously, dated, names of witnesses written in, parties who were apt to be interested; and after each case an amount in dollars set down with no notations about it. Jewels listed, husbands' incomes tabulated, and so on.

But I knew. This racket was old stuff to me. These amounts, ranging from a couple of thousand dollars up, were the amounts of blackmail that probably could be collected from interested parties. Small slips, small dough; big slips, plenty of cash. And I could see the girls losing their cash and signing their IOU's while their kitty-cat chatter about this one and that went down in cold black and white—stuff worth far more than the money they were losing over the tables every day.

How much of this dope, I wondered, had been used already? How many of those jewels, whose very hiding places were often written in, had been snatched? How many men had been faced with something they thought no one knew, told to lay it on the line in cash or take it on the front pages before their neighbors and friends? A small town where one's life has been spent is the place to crucify a man or woman. They've got so much to lose.

How many people had been whipped into mental anguish as great as Knapp's anguish when he turned to the Blaine Agency? I'd never know, of course. I don't think I wanted to know in that moment. Opening Benny's diary, I turned to the Middleton entries at the last and read.

And Benny's blond, grinning ghost stalked those pages of entries, filling the gaps I hadn't time to find. I've never believed in ghosts, but as I read that bold, angular, hasty handwriting Benny's finger pointed accusingly at the man who had killed him. It wasn't proof in court of law. I'd have to get that. But I knew what to do now; and I'd have to do it quick. It meant putting my own neck in a noose.

I put it.

A WRITING DESK stood in one corner of that dainty bedroom. In going through the desk I'd noticed some envelopes. In three of them I put the papers covering Knapp, addressed them to his office, stamped them with stamps from a book; and then picked up the telephone by the desk and called Knapp.

He must have been sitting beside his telephone.

I said, "Get your chief of police and a couple of his best detectives and come to the Chase woman's apartment. Arrest the big guy in the lobby and come up. I've got some stuff here I want you to see quickly."

Knapp stalled.

"Can't you bring it here?" he questioned.

"No."

"I—er—don't want the chief to know too much about this. Besides, he's looking for you. Harris, are you dithering?"

He finished that in a lather; and I said:

"I know they want me. That's my business. If you think the chief is crooked, bring someone whose word will be taken by everyone. This is important. Get me? Important!"

"I'll—I'll be there," Knapp said uncertainly.

Hanging up, I locked the tin box, carried it and the letters into the living room where Trixie was watching the French maid.

"You took long enough," Trixie sniffed.

"But what I found! Watch this box while I mail these letters."

I breathed easier when I dropped Knapp's business down the letter chute.

Trixie sniffed again when I locked the door behind me and rejoined them in the big room.

"You've got a nerve writing letters and mailing them," Trixie said. "What's next, setting-up exercises?"

I yawned. "Nothing," I said. "We'll make ourselves comfortable and see if Mabel will talk."

Would she? Nothing but cussing us both out every time I fired a question at her. That maid was tough when she wanted to be. Trixie finally said:

"You're wasting your breath, Ape. Don't you know anything better to do than this? What's in that tin box?"

"Papers."

"What kind of papers?"

"Show you after a while." And all the time I was listening for Knapp's arrival. God knows what was happening with the Chase woman out and her apartment closed to the public for the evening. Another murder at least, unless I missed my guess.

Then the bell buzzed quietly; and I went to the door and opened it on the chain—and the Chase woman herself was standing outside smiling at me.

"Please sir," she said. "Can I come into my apartment?"

Just like that. She knew I was in there, and she had come up alone. What else could I say than, "Step in. I've been waiting for you. No tricks."

She came in smiling, hands empty, without a purse. And a door at my right, from an empty, unused bedroom, snapped open. Trixie cried out: "Mike! Help!" And an automatic clipped me on the head as I turned, knocking me reeling, and I heard glass crash in the next room, and I dropped Trixie's automatic which I was dragging out.

11

CAPTIVES

HEAVEN WILL PROTECT the working girl, but I was only Mike Harris, red-headed dick. The light overhead was whirling, the walls were revolving, and I'll swear three tall thin men with automatics were jumping at me.

My head cleared before that army of gunmen reached me. It was only one man, raising his gun to clip me again. He looked as big as a house as I ducked, diving under the gun at his legs.

We crashed to the floor together. I think I could have taken him, but I didn't have a chance. He caught my right arm, hung on while he yelled something; then I saw that a second man had appeared and was hauling him off, rasping:

"Don't kill him, Slim!"

"I'll shoot his guts out! He's the one!" And as the fellow was dragged off me he snarled: "Lookit his red hair!"

That red top of mine again! I rolled, came to my knees warily, wondering if my ears were right. This Slim sounded like another Slim who had been killed in the room with me this same evening.

Then I saw the man who had pulled him off. Jack DeLand.

Square-shouldered, slim-hipped, handsome as ever, DeLand stood there panting slightly, another army automatic in his hand. He smoothed back slightly mussed hair with the palm of his hand, picked up the automatic I had dropped, spoke to me curtly.

"Get in the other room. Keep 'em up!"

And I kept 'em up. This Slim looked too hungry for a scalp. Tall, thin, wearing the same shoes and trousers I had seen from under the desk in DeLand's office, he stood there glaring. His hand squeezed the gun butt convulsively. I thought for a minute he was going to shoot me. His face was thin, angular, with cheekbones almost ridges, pale blond eyebrows over narrow-lidded eyes.

And I thought I must be dippy. One Slim was dead. The cops wouldn't be looking for me if he wasn't. Yet—here was the same fellow again. Same shoes, same pants, same name....

And Mabel, the French maid, was dancing on a tight wire. They had given her Trixie's gun. She was jabbing it in Trixie's back, smiling, having the time of her life.

"They came in from the back, Mike," Trixie said. "I was watching you—I didn't see them until it was too late."

"What did you throw through the window?" DeLand snapped.

"I wish it had been you," Trixie gave him back.

"Hardly the time to take that attitude, darling," the Chase woman said to her. "Celeste, what was it?"

One of the windows at this end of the room was broken out. "The box, *madame!*" Mabel says excitedly. "Your box! She t'row it out, so. *Voila!*"

"My box?"

"Oui! The box!"

"What?" And the Chase woman ran to the window, looked out, whirled. "Jack! Get it, quick! Oh, I could kill her for that!"

Ah, she was trim, chic, smart; but looking at her I thought of Benny Parker's dying words: "…watch brunette…" Poor Benny. He had known, had tried to warn me, and I had fumbled the deal. Looking into her pretty face, which was only beginning to show traces of recklessness, hardness, I knew that she meant her threat to Trixie; that for all of her we'd both get what Benny got.

WITH ANNOYANCE DE LAND said: "I can't get that damned box now. I told you not to keep it around here. Take a look at this man." He jerked his head at me.

She did, said slowly in a tight voice: "What are you doing here?"

No need to ask her what they were doing here, how they had surprised us. The Cossack downstairs must have tipped them off, and they had split—she coming up to draw attention, to the front door, the other two slipping in the back some way. No wonder she had been smiling and unconcerned as I let her in. I said: "I just dropped in."

And she cried: "That's the man, Jack! The same voice! I'd know it again!"

DeLand said: "I thought so. Just wanted to be sure. But I wonder what the Knapp girl had to do with this?" He bit his lip, scowled at me. "What about it?" he asked.

"Who said anything about such a woman?"

"Don't stall." He nodded at Trixie. "She used the Knapp girl's name downstairs."

"No law against using names, is there?"

That burnt him up. He jumped at me, grabbed me by the throat; and did that good looking bird have strength in his fingers? He did.

"Come on!" he snarled. "Talk fast. Who are you two? How did you ease in this? Where's Kennedy, damn you?"

I gagged when he released my throat. "How should I know about any Kennedy? Who is he?"

"You're lying, damn you! You were in my office when the two of you knocked Slim off!"

"There's Slim," I said.

And DeLand laughed; his weak, cruel month under the little mustache parted and showed white teeth as he laughed.

"Yes, there's Slim," he said. "And he'll kill you in a minute if I say the word. Spill it, fellow. Who are you? Both of you? And where's Kennedy?"

I should have felt a little easier, but I didn't. He didn't know I was a copper. Because he had heard I had been in his office when the killing happened, he thought I was working with Kennedy. The Chase woman, spotting me as the one she had stuck up in Benny Parker's room, still thought I was tied in with this Kennedy. So I was safe there; Trixie was safe there. And yet both of us were in just as bad because of the Kennedy angle. Anyone hooked with that fellow was small change around here. And what could I say but—

"Don't ask me where Kennedy is. I don't know. Why do you want him?"

DeLand showed his teeth again.

"Because," he said, "we're going to kill him before the

cops start him through the mill. He'll get it one way or the other, along with you—but we'll do it first."

The Chase woman said in the same tight voice:

"Kennedy is going to shoot the works. These two wouldn't have crashed the apartment if he wasn't. It's you or him, Jack."

And Slim said in a rasping snarl: "It'll be him!"

And I wondered where Mayor Knapp and his cops were. If they didn't get here quick, Trixie and I were ticketed for trouble. Heap trouble. It started a minute later. DeLand said:

"Kennedy won't be here. He'd have showed up if he was coming. Let's get these two out of here."

"My box!" the Chase woman said hastily.

"I'll see to it. Come on. These two were going to get in touch with Kennedy sometime tonight. We'll see that they do. Celeste, you stay here."

And out we went, guns in their pockets, smiles on their faces as they surrounded us in the elevator. In the lobby DeLand spoke under his breath to the big doorman, and out we went into a big sedan parked at the curb.

All the way down, clear into the car I had looked for Knapp and the cops. But they weren't there as we rolled away—speeding into oblivion where the cops and Knapp could be no good to us until it was too late....

12

A SCORE IS SETTLED

SLIM DROVE. TRIXIE sat between him and the Chase woman. In the back seat DeLand held a gun in my side; we had not gone half a mile before he said:

"You're going to talk, fellow."

"Yeah?"

"Yeah!" says DeLand—and his left fist smashed me in the side of the head.

Trixie cried: "Oh, Mike, I wish I could do something!"

She meant it. Game little Trixie, a gun in her own side, trapped in a mess I had gotten her into—and she was worrying about me. Head spinning, I straightened from the seat corner where DeLand had knocked me.

"The same to you if I ever get a chance," I told DeLand.

So he slugged me back in the corner again, keeping the gun hard against my ribs as a reminder of what I'd get if I lost my head.

"Where do we find Kennedy?" he demanded.

There was no percentage in taking his slugs all evening. I stalled him on the chance something would turn up. He wouldn't believe I didn't know anything about Kennedy.

"Why not try his house?" I suggested.

He knocked me over again.

"We did," he says through his teeth. "He wasn't there. Come on—where were you going to see him?"

I hurt. A ring on his finger had cut my cheek. Warm blood was coming out on the skin. I've heard about red anger. It came to me then as I straightened a third time; a crimson haze of fury which blurred eyesight for a moment, shook me in a tense, maniacal state in which I could have murdered. Then I got a grip on myself, said the first thing I could think of which seemed general enough to cover the case.

"Why not try his office?" I said.

"So?" says DeLand. "I wonder. We went past there and didn't see any sign of him. Slim, drive past Kennedy's store. Cruise around the block first and up the alley where he might have parked his car. We didn't look there."

"That's an idea," Slim agreed over his shoulder. "I'll take the alley first. I saw him driving outa there once. There's a parking place behind."

We went down town, turned into an alley, rolled quietly through; and halfway through Slim's voice cracked:

"There it is!"

SURE ENOUGH, BEHIND a building stood the car Trixie and I had followed from Jack's place. We rolled past, stopped in the next cross street.

"Slip back and watch that car and the back door, Slim," DeLand ordered. "There's no light in the back of the store, but he must be in there. Florence, you drive. I'll watch that wench beside you."

It was the first time he had called the Chase woman by name. Tight as the spot was, I thrilled. It confirmed the dope I had dug out. Slim left. The Chase woman drove us around the main drag, parked at the curb. The street looked lonely, deserted. They made us get out, walked us ahead several doors and stopped.

DeLand exclaimed: "There's a light behind the curtains now! He's in there! We've got him!" He jabbed me with the automatic. "Both of you step in the doorway there and knock until he lets you in. I'll be standing just beside the entrance. Crack wise to him and I'll drill you both!"

He meant it too. The next shop was a jewelry store. Curtains were drawn tight, lights showing dimly inside. The doorway was nearest us, the single show window on the other side. By standing flat against the building wall at my elbow DeLand would be invisible to anyone inside the jewelry store—and yet within arm's reach of my back, and Trixie's.

Under her breath Trixie sang softly: "Here I go picking posies," and stepped into that doorway and knocked on the door. And knocked—and kept on knocking until the light went out inside and a voice spoke on the other side of the door.

"Who is it?" the voice asked.

"Please let us in," Trixie begged.

The edge of the door curtain moved furtively. An eye surveyed us. Again Trixie begged: "Please, *please* let us in."

Of course he didn't know us. He must have been expecting cops or DeLand. I think he thought we were elopers, after one good gander at Trixie. She was so little, so sweet, so innocent when she pulled that line.

"Go away," the voice said gruffly. "This store is closed."

"But we must get in," Trixie insisted desperately. "It's

terribly important. You'll be sorry if you don't. This is Mr. Kennedy, isn't it?"

It was. Gruff as the voice was, I knew it. I don't know what DeLand thought of that crack of Trixie's. But it was a nice fat worm on a hook to Kennedy. Keyed up as he must have been, he was afraid to open the door and afraid to send Trixie away. For she might know something he'd better know. And we were strangers to him.

The door opened slightly.

"Come in," he said curtly. "But—be careful."

He had a gun of course. He was ready to use it—and what did I care if he did as long as we got safely in past him? For DeLand was behind us and he'd draw any fire. Maybe they'd kill each other off. But—

Poppp behind my shoulder. And I shoved Trixie hard, carrying her through the darkness away from that door, away from the gasp, the choke, the little spreading cloud of hell which had been turned loose just behind my back, I'd heard that *poppp* before in other places. I knew what it meant. Someone—DeLand of course—had reached in and fired one of those little pen gas guns at Kennedy's person. It ruined him right there.

Feet scuffled, the door slammed, Kennedy was choking and cursing—and as Trixie and I reached the back of the store safe from the gas, a light went on. DeLand was standing midway back, away from the gas also, with a gun in his hand. Kennedy was clawing a handkerchief over eyes blinded with tears.

KENNEDY HAD DROPPED his gun. The agony in his eyes blotted out everything else as he staggered back from that pocket of gas by the door.

"Back this way to your office," DeLand clipped out. "The air will be all right there."

Kennedy stopped short in his agony. "Who's that?"

"DeLand. Who else?"

"I thought it was the police!" Kennedy sobbed in his hoarse choking voice; and docility fell over him like a smothering blanket and he groped a helpless way to the back.

DeLand was grinning under his little mustache. He was still grinning as he turned on the light in the back room, unlocked a door there, let in Slim and the Chase woman, who must have made for the back as soon as DeLand entered.

The front room had gleamed with silver, gold, jewelry in polished floor cases and wall cases. This back room was small, plain, with a safe against the wall, an open desk holding a telephone and papers across from it, and a single small table covered with black velvet standing in the middle of the floor under a shaded light. On the table was an open traveling bag.

DeLand looked in it and chuckled. I've never heard a nastier sound.

"Getting ready to beat it, eh, Kennedy?" he said, and he reached down in the bag and picked up a handful of rings, bracelets, necklaces. The shaded light glinted, gleamed, glittered on diamonds, pearls, emeralds as DeLand strewed them on the black velvet.

Slim had a gun on me. I had backed against the desk, and I stood there with my hands behind me watching, listening. There was no gas in here. Kennedy's red-rimmed eyes looked horrible as he pawed his handkerchief futilely at them, gasping:

"Why shouldn't I get out, DeLand? You were going to kill me. I don't want trouble."

"You mean," said DeLand, "you couldn't find me to kill me, so you got yellow and thought you'd run with everything you could get your hands on!"

The safe door was open; the inner door open. Little drawers were pulled out and scraps of tissue paper littered the floor, where they had been dropped after their contents had been taken. Unset stones, probably.

"No," choked Kennedy.

But Slim spoke viciously. "He's a damn liar! Look at that bag!"

"Sure, Slim. We all know he's lying," DeLand said.

And Kennedy froze in his agony, his head cocked toward Slim, his sightless, streaming eyes staring.

"My God, who's that?" he said.

Slim said harshly: "Who'd you think?"

"But—but—"

"But hell!" Slim rasped. "You killed one Slim: at Jack's place tonight You and this red-headed punk by the desk there. So you can't figure Slim here, huh?"

"I never saw any red-head," Kennedy denied. Sweat was running down his face.

"You just let him in!" Slim snapped.

"Th-that man? I never saw him before. Or the woman with him either."

And DeLand said wonderingly: "I believe he's right. They didn't talk like it out front." He turned to me, upper lip drawing back against his teeth. "Who are you?" he rapped out.

And I laughed at him.

"I'm a dick," I said. "Mike Harris, from the Blaine Agency. This is Trixie Meehan, who's working with me. I've been looking for the man who killed Benny Parker— and I've found him. It would be funny if there were *two* Slims, wouldn't it? One who worked for you publicly, DeLand, and another no one knew anything about. Two twin brothers, who could manage to be one place, yet have a perfect alibi before reputable witnesses in the other. It's been worked before. The tall man who shot Benny Parker at the city hall this afternoon and got away, couldn't have been convicted by witnesses."

KENNEDY BEGAN TO laugh; ghastly, gasping chuckles. "Detectives, DeLand! From the Blaine Agency! So they got you anyway?"

"Got me?" said DeLand "I guess not. I brought them here. I've got you all now. I had one of these Blaine Agency dicks knocked off because he got to you, some-way, Kennedy. Slim here did it. I don't know how much you told. I gave you a break to get out of town, but you couldn't leave the soft spot I'd put you in. You wanted the dough you'd been making, wanted a fist deeper in the soft spot I've made here in Middleton. So you shot my man, the other Slim—this Slim's brother. You figured with him out of the way and me out of the way you'd have a break, the kind of a break you wanted, everything. Slim is going to take care of you, Kennedy. He cared a lot for that brother of his you gunned. I thought this dick did it at first, while you were in my office with Slim. But if you never saw this man before, he wasn't there. I know you were. Slim went in there with you. I told him to, saw him start there with you. And if this red-head is a cop he wouldn't have stood for a killing there."

DeLand laughed this time.

"When the cops came to my place," he said, "I didn't mention you, Kennedy. I wanted you first. They'll be surprised when they find you in a ditch. They'll wonder who killed the new jeweler. I'll leave a couple of things around here, so they'll get wise you've been fencing stuff. They'll figure you've crooked someone, and got knocked off for it. Not a bonehead in the whole department will have an idea I brought you here and gave you a front and worked through you. How does that sound, Kennedy?"

Kennedy peered at them. He was a plain looking man, bigger than DeLand; but in that moment his face was desperate, haggard, twisted with emotion. I guess he knew his ace card had been turned up and he had lost. He didn't have a chance—so he took a chance, diving at DeLand who was nearest. God, I've never seen anything like that jump right into their guns, knowing he was going to die—and not giving a damn.

13

THE PHANTOM WITNESS

DELAND SHOT HIM first. The blasting shot almost deaf-ened me. I saw Kennedy jerk as the bullet struck him—but he was on DeLand an instant later, tearing at his gun with the strength of a crazy man, turning it away so the next shot tore harmlessly into the wall.

They knocked the table over and diamonds and pearls cascaded to the floor. And Slim, looking murderous and wild, danced around and shoved his gun against Kennedy's side and pulled the trigger.

I was coming away from the desk in that instant with a paperweight in my hand. A heavy, glass gadget. I hadn't been ready for suicide, but this called the turn on every-thing. Now that the killing had started it would keep up until the end.

Slim pulled the trigger again as I slammed the paper-weight at him. My ringing ears couldn't catch the sodden impact—but Slim spun on a heel and went down inertly, dropping his gun.

Kennedy, shot to pieces, was going down also; but going down fighting, clinging to DeLand's gun with the last dying frenzy of hate. I don't think he could see; I doubt if he knew what he was doing; but he was rendering the cursing, fighting DeLand helpless for an instant more while I reached them.

DeLand's gun went off again, just missing me; and cuddling that paperweight in the palm of my hand I slammed it over the top of Kennedy's sinking head. It struck full in the middle of DeLand's face, pulping those pretty features into a mess. A rhinoceros would have dropped before that blow. DeLand did. His pretty face would never be the same again.

And when I turned there was Trixie backing the Chase woman against the wall. Trixie, with a gun in her hand and the Chase woman with a scratched face and her hair hanging loose where Trixie had stormed all over her.

"The cat drew a gun and tried to mix in," Trixie panted.

"Baby!" I yelled. "You're God's gift to a dumb dick! Hold her!"

"What do you think I'm doing, Ape?" Trixie gave me cheerfully—and just at that moment glass crashed in the front of the store and the back door smashed in as if an elephant were coming through.

Then coppers, swarms of them, crowding into the office and store. I've never seen so many coppers sprout in a few moments. The chief was there, the big dick I had punched in the jaw, and Mayor Knapp, red-faced and excited.

"Are we in time?" Knapp hollered.

"We're serving cake for the next course," I told him. "Sit down and sharpen your teeth."

BUT MORGAN, THE chief of police, was like a terrier who had fallen into a rat's nest. His nose was fairly quivering as he sniffed the powder laden air and looked at the casualties on the floor.

"Call an ambulance!" he ordered one of his men. "Get a doctor here as quickly as you can!" And he shoved his fist at me. "Harris, I've been looking for you! I wanted you for murder—and by heavens you pull off a stunt like this! How did you know what was going to happen? Why didn't you leave word for us to come here?" He snorted. "I ought to throw you in a cell for stirring up a rumpus like this!"

"We—we didn't know whether we could get here in time or not," Knapp stuttered. He looked like a man who had run through a wringer. He said: "To think this man Kennedy was a crook. He had joined the Chamber of Commerce. Who—who shot him?"

And Trixie's jaw was sagging.

"Will you tell me," she asks, "how you know so much that we just found out? Were you listening outside?"

Morgan, the chief of police, didn't look so hard as he towered over little Trixie.

"We just got here," he said. "But all the way here we were getting broadcasts about what was happening in here. I've never seen this new-fangled radio equipment used so fast and so successfully."

"You were hearing what happened in here?" Trixie bleated. "Is this place a broadcasting station?" She looked around the room, and the Chase woman did, too.

"Some day you'll learn all the tricks," I told Trixie kindly. "While I was standing there at the desk I lifted the receiver behind me. Everything that was said here was going out over the telephone. I figured the operator at this time of the night would hear enough to make her call the cops. I guess she did."

"She did!" the Chief snapped. "Everything said in here

has been taken down on wax records at headquarters. They hooked the line on one of the new recording machines we've been testing. And as fast as it came in they shot it out over the air to us, while the patrol cars all closed in to this store."

THAT GOT A sigh of relief from me. A lot that had been said in here wouldn't have been proof in court. But a wax record would. Off my shoulders right then rolled the burden of proof that I was a killer. And I said:

"There's a box at the apartment house that Miss Meehan threw out the window."

"We've got it," the Chief said promptly. "The doorman was just coming in with it when we got there and arrested him. Haven't had a chance to see what's inside."

"I'll tell you," I said. "And get ready for a shock. DeLand was plenty crook, playing for big stakes. He'd done a turn in St. Quentin. When he got out a society girl by the name of Florence Hughes fell hard for him, eloped with him. Her family tried to stop it. The mess got in the papers. His real name was Charles Sands. You'll find the dope under those names in the newspaper morgues in Frisco. There is Florence Hughes."

The Chase girl was white, biting her lower lip. She said to me: "How did you know that?" I think shame for the disgrace she was bringing on her family was getting her down fast now.

"Got it all over telegraph and telephone lines from Frisco today," I said. "First about DeLand, or Sands. He's from around Middleton here. I had the records at Quentin searched for a crook connected with this section. They put the finger on Sands right away. You were hooked up with him. I got your address book, which had lots of big names from the Pacific coast in it. Plain you had been somebody once, and had met Sands out there. The papers should have had something about it—and they did."

Knapp was moistening his lips. He didn't know what was coming yet. The chief's eyes were boring at me as I went on—

"These two came here, got some money, started that roadhouse. But DeLand is the only one who appeared there. His wife opened up a neat little apartment, began to catch the smart women of town in a gambling racket.

"That was only part of the deal, though. Blackmail was the big card. The women talked, and all of it went down to be used when needed. DeLand—I'll call him that since you all know him by that name—made more and more money, began to mix in with politics and intrench firmly. No one suspected he was crooked, or had an idea he was bringing other crooks in to work for him—as he did Kennedy here, setting him up in business to fence stolen things. Kennedy is an old time fence, who had to fade out of Chicago. But he had contacts; he was valuable.

"Not," I said, "until Mayor Knapp was threatened with blackmail was anything done about it. And then he hired a man out of his own pocket from the Blaine Agency."

Knapp looked like he was ready to faint. He thought it was all coming out now.

The chief snapped: "What? Mayor Knapp threatened with blackmail? And we knew nothing about it? What did they have on you, Your Honor?"

Knapp opened his mouth soundlessly.

They all had their ears spread, waiting for a juicy morsel. And I said smoothly:

"Knapp's daughter had been so foolish as to lose money in a crooked card game and gave her IOU. She was afraid to tell her father, couldn't pay the debt. So they threatened him, thinking it would get him in bad with the church element if it got out his daughter had gambled. Like a patriotic citizen," I told that gang with all organ stops out and a throb in my voice, "Mayor Knapp refused to be blackmailed. He called in a detective agency and told them to go ahead.

SURE, I LIED a little. Knapp had asked the Blaine Agency to protect him. Our first duty was to him. And you could see Knapp coming to life, getting the drift that maybe he had a chance after all.

"We could have done it better," Morgan said ungraciously.

"Sure you could have, chief. Only the mayor was afraid there might be a leak. You were to get the dope we turned up; only things broke so fast when they started, there wasn't time. Our man was killed today, as he was going into give the mayor what information he had to date. I had just gotten in town. I never did get that dope until I turned it up in this woman's apartment.

"Parker, our man who was killed, kept a diary. I knew that. No one else did. I went to his room at the Century Hotel looking for that diary."

"Are you the guy who sloughed me on the jaw?" Murphy, the big dick, yelled.

"Brother," said sadly, "that hurt me more than it did you. I'm so little and you're so big I didn't figure it'd hurt you. All

I wanted was a chance to get out the window before you nabbed me. I couldn't afford to be questioned right then."

One of his brother dicks snickered. He took the cue, rubbed his jaw, allowed: "You may be little but you pack a wallop. Okay. Forget it."

"You see," I went on, "DeLand's wife had been in the room when I entered. She stuck me up, locked me up and scrammed. I had just gotten out when you came. She had that diary. I wanted it; but I didn't get it until I looked in that tin box you have. It's in there; and when you look in it you'll see how Parker came to town, spotted Kennedy, recognized him, and took a room at the Century and played a crook. Then he put pressure on Kennedy, got an insight into Kennedy's dealings with DeLand, and how DeLand was tying in with all the crooked elements in town. It's all there. Some way DeLand got wise, decided to stop Parker, and just caught him at the mayor's office. I guess they were pretty desperate to risk that. DeLand was in the soup then. He had to keep on, stop everyone who was dangerous to him. He tried it—and there he is; it'll take a little time to unravel everything, but you've got your case."

"And what a case!" said the chief.

The ambulance got there just then, doctors, action; and I got Knapp aside and told him what was coming through the mail.

"All the evidence is in the mail," I said. "I think we can keep your history quiet. The Chase woman may know and try to talk, but she's in no position to be listened to. DeLand evidently snatched all the records."

"I don't see how you traced him, Harris."

"Easy. He had to be from around this section to spot

your mug in those St. Quentin records and know the data might be worth something to him. I worked back from that. And Benny's diary didn't say what he came here for. You're safe on that."

Knapp had tears in his eyes; yes, tears of relief.

"Harris," he says, "I'll never forget this."

"Neither will I," I told him. "I've never been so close to hysteria as on this case. Here I come to catch a crook and almost get tried for murder myself. All I want is to get back to New York. You can have your quiet, peaceful little town."

So I rode back to New York with Trixie. So sweet, so helpless. What a woman!

www.ingramcontent.com/pod-product-compliance
Lightning Source LLC
Chambersburg PA
CBHW030532030726
47495CB00004B/959